Calla Falling

TALLIE ROSE

www.tallierose.com
Twitter: _tallierose
Instagram: _tallierose

| One |

ONCE upon a time Calla had been extraordinary. She'd had the world's coolest job, a calling, a purpose, a secret identity. Not anymore. Tonight it was just her and her salad. From now on she was only going to order drinks. A drink was cheaper, took less time. She could get up and leave without embarrassing herself by waiting for a date who wasn't going to show.

Again.

One guy had stood up as soon as he found out she was a hunter, straightened his dinner jacket, placed his napkin on the table and said, "Not worth the trouble." Another time she thought she was having a great evening with a beautiful woman until she went to the bathroom and never came back, like something out of a sitcom but without the laugh track.

Having her date not show up was almost a blessing—better than someone leaving halfway through. If she didn't glance at the door too often, people would just think she was having dinner alone.

The waiter came over, a look of mock sympathy plastered across his face. "Another glass of wine?"

"No, thanks." She smiled just enough that he would leave.

What was she doing? For the last eight months, she'd been falling apart. She didn't need to be dating. She needed to figure out exactly what she was going to do with her life now that everything had changed. But she didn't know how to let go, how to be a different person. A less angry person.

Maybe she would move. Start over in a new place. Make some new friends. Get a normal job. New Dunwich had once been her home but just like the entire world it had turned into a stranger.

She used to walk the streets like she owned them, now there were signs of vampires everywhere. And not the way it had once been, not the signs only the hunters could see. Literal signs. Freaking billboards of vampires.

And where did that leave Calla? A predator without prey. Though she hadn't done well in biology, she knew how that ended. Death. Extinction.

She pulled out some cash and put it on the table. She couldn't stand another moment in this restaurant. Her body was tingling, eight months of wanting to fight and having no adversary. There were only so many punching bags she could hit. She wanted to stake something. Anything.

Vampires had joined society, so what? They still drank blood. They were still demons in human skin. Her phone vibrated in her pocket and she silenced it. Probably the Council again, trying to get her to agree to one thing or another. They wanted her out front, speaking about peace and love. *With fucking bloodsuckers.* She didn't want to be their spokeswoman. She did need their money, though, so she could only duck their calls for so long.

She wasn't sure where she was going, but the city was just coming to life. The street lights overhead blinked on, brightening the balmy night. Calla scanned the street, searching the shadows.

Sighing, Calla shoved her hands in her pocket. She couldn't turn her instincts off, but she wished she could stop *thinking* about it. She'd thought about vampires less when she was killing them than now. Her only balm was that she knew she was not the only one who felt the way she did. Plenty of humans agreed with her, she got mail every day. *Keep up the good work. Stake 'em good, baby. Bloodsuckers never change.*

Maybe bloodsuckers never changed but the world sure had. She turned a corner and came face to face with an enormous poster of Isolde. Blonde, beautiful, dead for hundreds of years. No last name, like Cher. Calla pulled the poster off the wall and shoved it into the nearest trash can.

"Hey!"

She turned towards the voice. "What?" Her hand went to her hip, but her stake wasn't there. God, she missed her stake.

"She's doing a book signing. Don't tear that down. It was expensive."

Calla ground her teeth together. "Oh, well, I wouldn't want to ruin a vampire's all-you-can-eat-buffet." She pulled the crumbled poster out of the garbage and threw it at the woman as her phone vibrated again. Without listening to the rest of the tirade being launched her way, she started walking, pulling her phone out of her pocket. Her best friend's name flashed across the screen.

"Hey Lisbet. He didn't show."

"Forget about that. Haven't you checked your email?" There was an urgency in Lisbet's voice that sent adrenaline rushing through Calla.

"No." Calla ducked into the nearest alley. "What's going on?"

"It's your mom. She...well, she killed Estienne."

"Who the fuck is Estienne?" But there was a familiarity to the name, something she couldn't place.

"He's some kind of important vampire.. I don't—fuck, Calla." Lisbet lowered her voice, hissing into the phone. "I know it's what we do. I want to kill them too, but they caught her. The vampires are furious and so is the Council. If this blows up we're fucked."

Calla slid down the brick wall behind her until her ass hit the grimy pavement. Her mother had always been rash, quick to act. She needed to be. She fought vampires. Acting before thinking kept you alive. She had always known she would lose her mother, vampire hunters rarely died of old age, but to lose her like this? She couldn't watch her rot away behind bars. Not for this. Anger, white and hot, flared through her.

"Calla…"

Before she could answer another call came in. A number she didn't recognize. "I should take this." She hung up, her mind somehow both blank and racing. "Hello?"

"Hello Ms. Chase. Are you available to meet and discuss your mother? Twenty minutes at the Council headquarters?"

She didn't recognize the voice on the other end of the phone and she knew everyone on the Council. "Who is this?" She pushed herself to her feet. This was no time to fall apart. She needed to think, to be the person she was raised to be.

"I'm a representative for the vampires. Can you meet Ms. Chase or shall we go ahead and charge your mother?"

"I'll be there." She hung up, hands shaking.

Calla barely saw the city as she raced through it. People yelled as she knocked into them, and she banged her elbow on a park bench, but she didn't slow her pace. Her mother, the esteemed Delphine Chase, one of the greatest vampire hunters in several generations was being held somewhere and the Council was in on it.

The thought deflated her, turning her rage into sorrow. She wanted to be mad at the Council, to tear the building down brick by brick but those people had raised her. That building had been her second home. While her mother was out hunting, she would roam the halls, sit in on trainings, steal from the kitchens, practice fighting in empty classrooms. She'd met Lisbet in the Council building.

How could they do this to her? Another piece of the puzzle that made up who she was had been ripped away. Another hole in her soul.

She rounded a corner, barely keeping herself from tripping and the Council building came into view. She started towards the door and halted when her least favorite person came into view. Finally, something she knew how to do. Hating Gus was familiar, comfortable.

"Good evening, Calla." He ran a hand through his dark hair. Smarmy. Calla had punched him once when she was nine. The memory still warmed her. But now she was too old for hitting people who were, technically, not any worse than irritating.

"Good for whom, Gus?" She tried to move past him, uninterested in whatever his answer would be, but he stepped in front of the double doors, blocking her path.

"Wait. Seriously, Calla. The Council is...." He sighed. "They need a scapegoat and your mom just offered herself up on a silver platter. Whatever our differences, we are working towards the same thing."

Except she wasn't sure they were anymore. And that was what hurt the most. The change in the Council had made her hollow and now the desire to hunt vampires, once so strong, rattled around in her chest. "I need to go see my mother."

"That's why I'm out here. You aren't seeing your mother, Calla. And I urge you to say no. She made her decisions. It doesn't mean they have to be yours. You don't have to do this."

A chill ran down Calla's spine. It wasn't like Gus to break with the Council, but it wasn't like her either. But he was still Gus, and she didn't need to talk about this with him anymore or she would walk into the building with his ideas in her head. "Okay." She moved forward firmly, brushing past him and pushed open the double doors.

The familiar scent of the Council building hit her nose, bringing memories rushing back. She squared her shoulders. She was Calla Chase, the latest hunter in a long line of world class hunters. Whatever was happening she would handle it, like she'd handled everything else that had come her way.

Calla took a moment before she went deeper into the building to smooth her dark hair and straighten her clothes. She had no idea what she was walking into. Better to look as put together as she could manage.

Heels clicked on the polished marble floor, and Naomi appeared from around a corner. Though her age was finally starting to show, Naomi was still a striking woman, with dark hair and sharp features. She'd trained Calla's mother, and while she was not a warm person, she'd done great things since she'd joined the board of the Council. "Calla. I hate seeing you under these circumstances."

Calla nodded. "Is my mother okay?"

"Delphine is as well as she could be, all things considered. Can you please follow me?" Naomi didn't wait for an answer. She turned and headed back down the hallway she had appeared from, and Calla had no choice but to follow.

Fear continued to tighten its grip. "Naomi, I got a call from a vampire. What is going on?"

Naomi stopped and turned back towards Calla, a look she'd never seen before on her face. "What's going on is, we're doing the best we can," she hissed. "You know we had no plans for this, we never expected the vampires to make their presence known to the world. And you and your mother have refused, at every opportunity, to work with us."

"Of course we don't want to work with you to create peace with the vampires." Calla wanted to scream, wanted to hit something.

"You foolish girl. What *do* you want? Chaos? Have you even thought of the consequences if the vampires get personhood? How many of them have you killed? And of those, how many were a direct danger to you? What do you plan to say when you're sitting in front of a jury? Self defense for homes you broke into? For stakings you did while the vampire slept?"

"They're monsters, Naomi."

"I know that. I have given my life to this organization, but we have to find a way to cope with this, to move forward. Eventually the world will learn what we already know, but until then we have to rise above. So keep an open mind, please." She seemed to strain to say the last word, and Calla wasn't sure she'd ever heard her say it before.

"Fine. But can someone tell me what's going on? You've never led me into an ambush, surely you don't mean to start now."

Naomi's face softened. "You are meeting with the vampire Isolde. You may remember her as the member of the Directorate who led to their outing. She has told us little of what she wants to say to you, except that she wants to come to an understanding to help your mother. She walked in here and demanded we give her your number." Naomi moved closer. "Calla, Delphine could rot in jail for this. They could make an example out of her. I urge you to listen to what she has to say. Try to see the vampire as something other than an adversary. We've all been forced to do it."

Calla took a deep breath, steadying her thoughts. Her mother was in trouble. That was what she needed to focus on. Not her anger at the vampires. Not her frustration with the Council. She couldn't imagine what was coming next, but if she went in with anger, it wouldn't be the vampires she was hurting, it would be her mother. It would be all the innocent people who would be further duped by the monsters who walked among them. The monsters who no longer had anyone standing in their path.

"Okay. I'm ready."

Naomi smiled. "I can see that. Your training hasn't completely abandoned you. We'll get through the weeds. One day at a time. One fight at a time."

Calla nodded. "One fight at a time."

"Okay. Follow me." Naomi squeezed Calla's shoulder and led her to the hall they kept furnished for visitors. One foot in front of the other. One breath and then another. Calla's world was changing, and for the first time she realized she had to change with it or she would be swept away in the rising tide.

Vampires would always be the enemy, but there was more than one way to fight. Fists and stakes did not always do the trick. She'd known that all her life. Being a vampire hunter felt like part of her identity, but it was a costume she wore, something safe she draped herself in. It was time to don a new costume. To find a new way to fight.

Naomi stopped in front of a door and turned, putting her hands on Calla's shoulders. "Your mother has always been one of our best hunters and you are just as strong as she is. We have eyes on the room. You will be safe."

"Don't make promises you can't keep."

"Then the truth. None of us are safe, Calla. These are unprecedented times. But you are with the Council, and no matter how you rage against us, we are family." Naomi put a fist to her chest and Calla did the same.

"Wish me luck." Calla winked and turned the doorknob.

| Two |

CALLA knew what she would find when she opened the door, but the sight of such an ancient vampire still took her breath away. Her fingers went to her side, to the stake she had put away months ago but not yet forgotten the feeling of. She was a hunter and here was her prey. But no longer.

Isolde was undeniably gorgeous. Sheets of long blonde hair framed her face and fell in waves to her waist. She looked like an old movie star, with red lips and wide brown eyes, lined with thick lashes. Her dress was strange, heavy fabric with embroidery down the sides. Vampires never quite figured out how to fit in.

"Come, sit." Isolde gestured to one of the four chairs in the room.

"I'd rather not."

"Must we start this way? Snarling at each other?"

"I simply declined. That is not snarling."

Isolde grinned, her sharp incisors on full display. "Fine. Well, Calla, I have a proposition for you. You won't like it, but I urge you to listen."

"I'm all ears, *Isolde.*" Calla hated not knowing what was coming. She liked details, to have a plan, to always be sure-footed. This was unfamiliar territory, and she was entirely off kilter. Worst of all, the vampire knew it.

Isolde sat in one of the overstuffed armchairs, crossing one leg over the other. Calla had seen many people sit in that chair over the years, dignitaries, world leaders, and foreign hunters. But never a vampire. She gritted her teeth while Isolde continued to smile. "I really wish you would sit."

"Fine." Calla sat across from her, hands on her knees, ready to pounce. She didn't trust for a moment that the Council would get there in time if Isolde attacked her, but she trusted herself.

"Well, to get down to it, your mother killed a high-ranking vampire. And I'm certain you don't care about that, but it was all on video. Obviously, she didn't know anyone was there. Still, it's reckless for a hunter. I'm also certain you also don't want to hear that. But Estienne was an old vampire, not as old as I am, but he had lived for centuries. And he always had a soft spot for humans. An aggressive vampire might not have set the Directorate quite so much on edge. But sweet Estienne?" She clucked her tongue.

Calla's fingers tightened on her knees.

"Again, why should you care? Except, as you and I both know, the human government is in chaos. They don't know what to do with us. And they don't know what to do with you."

"Agreed," Calla said between gritted teeth.

"Well, that's a start. So I see a few options of how the future will go. Maybe humans will accept vampires. They've always loved tales of us and if we can drink non-human and synthetic blood, they might come around. Then they will not care for the hunters and you will have no mission. Some might even see you as murderers—you know how most humans are. Gullible. That is what the Directorate wants."

"And you? You are the reason your kind is known." Where was this going? Calla couldn't begin to imagine.

"I'll get to that later. The other way our future could play out would be for humans to hate us. If they hate us, they will love the hunters. You'll be heroes. Seen as you are, protecting the humans. But, Calla, do you think that is how it will go?"

"No." It was the truth, however much she hated it.

"Indeed. It seems unlikely. But even if it goes as the Directorate wants, there will be those against us. There will be fights and legal battles and so much trouble. I'd like a middle ground. And I thought, in exchange for us letting your mother go, forgiving her completely, you might be compelled to work with us. To work with me." Isolde pushed her hair over her shoulder. She reminded Calla of a marble statue, smooth and unblemished. Ageless and timeless.

"This is all very vague."

Isolde laughed like a ringing bell. Everything about her was just shy of human. Her accent was nothing Calla could identify, or perhaps she did not have one at all. The turning of time had washed away every trace of the person she had once been.

"I suppose it is. But the vampires are willing to change. In fact, we have been working towards change for some time. We drink from donors, not victims. Some do not drink from humans at all. The way we lived before was cruel and always unsustainable. As the world became more connected, we were bound to be caught."

"You haven't changed," Calla interrupted. "You were caught attacking a human. That's what started all this."

For the first time since Calla had come into the room, Isolde's face changed. A glance of something beneath the marble surface. "Believe me, that man deserved to die. But you are sharp, so let me be frank with you. The Directorate is angry with me. I have until the solstice to sway human opinion."

"Or...?"

"Or there will be consequences. But I can not change people's opinion on my own. Right now no one outside of the Council and Directorate knows what your mother did. It can stay that way. But you can help me change their opinion. Look at you, you would do well on camera. Humans would love you. So you must make them love me too, and in return your mother will be spared, vampires will behave and the Council will not have to worry about any consequences for all the murders—however justified—they have committed."

Calla wanted to smash something. Make the world love vampires? It turned her stomach. "What about all the murders vampires have committed?"

"Do you have any on film that I am unaware of?"

No, she didn't. And Isolde knew it. They had never needed justification for their slayings, and it was safer to not record footage at all. "How would I even do what you're asking?"

The vampire readjusted the thick green fabric of her skirt, leaning closer to Calla. "We will make them believe we have a... friendship. That you have found something in me you find enjoyable and loveable. If fierce vampire hunter Calla Chase can find a way to love the vampires, the rest of the humans are sure to follow along. You will come to events with me, be seen with me, you will speak on my behalf. As long as you cooperate, the rules will be enforced, humans will be safe. Your mother will be safe. Of course, you will help get the Council in line. While they cooperate currently, they do not care for us. We need to know we are safe as well."

Calla stood and paced the room, her thoughts racing. What Isolde asked was against everything she believed in, everything she had been taught. "I have no control over the Council or their opinions. I do not sit on the board, none of my family has ever sat on the board. That is a promise I simply can not make."

Isolde nodded. "Understood. You are a soldier, not a leader."

The truth of her words was sharp, cutting like a knife into Calla's deepest fears. "And if I don't agree?"

"If you don't agree, I will share the tape of your mother with the proper authorities. I will show her attacking a man who was doing nothing more than walking. I will demand retribution and settle for nothing less than her execution. Estienne sat on the board of several charities. He has dozens of humans that will speak to his kindness and generosity. The battle will not be hard and I will not stop. And if I fail at winning the human's sympathy, then I will go down knowing that I brought a hunter with me."

Calla lashed out, smashing a vase against the wall. Beneath it, water spread across the red carpet, turning it crimson. Isolde didn't even flinch. "Fine," Calla said, hating herself for it.

"Perfect." Isolde clapped her hands together and stood. "You will move into my manor. I'm sure—"

"Move into your manor?" It took all of Calla's restraint not to scream. "Why in the fuck would I—You want them to think we're lovers!"

"It is the easier sell, Calla. Friends? Friendship takes time, trust. But passion? That takes moments." She stepped closer. "A heated look. Just a smile."

Isolde was closer than any vampire had been to Calla without death on the horizon. Calla could smell her perfume, see the freckles across her nose, a dusting of color against her pale skin. "And what good will it do if they think I'm the idiot hunter fucking a vampire?"

"Perhaps they think that at first, but you will sell it. Maybe they believe we are in love. Fools always believe love means something. They will see your devotion to me, your commitment, and they will think that if you can find love in your heart, certainly they can find acceptance."

Calla took another step closer. The vampire's skirt brushed her legs. "As old as you are, I assumed you were smart, but this is the plan of a fool."

Again, the vampire's face changed, fury flashing behind her brown eyes. "What do you know of humans? Have you ever been in love, Calla? Have you ever had a friend who was not a hunter? You think they are like you, but they are not. They are fickle and easily swayed. I am seven hundred years old. I did not live this long without understanding humans. But if you dislike my plan, simply say so."

"You know I can't."

"Then stop arguing."

Every fiber of Calla's body screamed at her. This was foolish. She was walking into a trap. But she knew the vampire would do as she said. She would make an example of Calla's mother. Each day backed Calla further into a corner, wearing down the parts of her that made up her identity, eroding the lies she told herself about who she was. And who *would* she be when all the sharp edges were gone? What would be left?

She wanted to drive a stake deep into Isolde's heart, to watch the surprise in her eyes, the way her skin would wither as she fell to the floor. But the cost was too high. "I'll do what you ask, but don't make me live with you."

"I am not negotiating, little hunter. I intend to keep an eye on you. Just as I did not make it this long without knowing humans, I did not live this long without recognizing a threat. You do not fall in line easily. I see the hatred in your eyes. I will not leave you alone to scheme and plan with your mother." Isolde reached forward, and her touch chilled Calla to the bone. She pushed a strand of Calla's hair behind her ear. "I will have you to myself. You may even find you like it."

Calla swallowed hard. "Okay. But answer me this, how did you make it so long and yet still get caught?"

Isolde smiled. "It was bound to happen to one of us. I was driven by anger and not by intelligence. I would explain myself, but you would not listen, so I will not waste my breath. Perhaps when we have spent some time together, I will tell you all there is to know."

Calla could still feel Isolde's fingers on her skin. "It will be a long time before I believe anything you have to say."

Isolde stepped back. "Believe what you want, Calla. I will have your things moved to my house." And in a flurry of blonde hair and rustling fabric, Isolde slipped through the door.

| Three |

BEFORE the door fully closed, it opened again, and Lisbet was rushing through it. "Girl..." She flopped into an armchair and Calla did the same. "What the fuck?"

"This is fucked up. This is so so so fucked up." Calla raked her fingers through her hair. How could she live with a vampire? "Lisbet, this is so completely fucked up. I can't do this. I seriously can't do this." Her heart pounded in her chest and she couldn't catch her breath.

Lisbet leaned closer and glanced towards a corner, where Calla was sure a camera was hidden. She cleared her throat. "Come on." She put out her hand and Calla took it, allowing her best friend to lead her through the hallways of the Council and back into the open air. Neither of them spoke until they were well clear of the building.

"Breathe," Lisbet commanded

Calla tried. She inhaled. How many more moments did she have like this? How long until she traded her own freedom for her mother's? She exhaled. Her heart rate slowed and her panic subsided.

"They were going to allow your mom to be the sacrificial lamb. The entire council is floundering. You did the only thing you could."

"What do we do?" She glanced back towards the Council building. How could this have happened? She almost expected to see Naomi rushing out, begging her not to do this, but no one did. A hunter's life was not their own. They worked for the greater good. But how could this be good?

Lisbet followed her gaze, and her face fell. "I don't know, Calla. I really don't. I've spent my whole life listening to the Council. Sure, sometimes I argued, but I believed in what we were doing. Now, I don't know what to believe in."

Calla walked until she found a bench, until she was too far to see the building she was growing to hate. She sat, and the metal was cool against her legs. She tried to let the chill ground her and keep her thoughts from running away too fast and too far. "If I pretend to be in love with a vampire, then I'm no better than them. I'm lying to the world."

Lisbet didn't look at her, her gaze somewhere over Calla's shoulder, and it broke Calla's heart. "Just do what you need to do to survive, and we'll come up with a plan. We'll get you out of this. And don't blame yourself, you didn't have a choice."

Calla nodded, but she wasn't sure that was true. She could have refused. They'd vowed to give their life to the cause, to live for nothing else, but as soon as her vows had been tested she'd chosen her mother over her beliefs. "They were supposed to be our leaders, Lis, but they didn't plan for this."

"Don't attack me for this, but how could they? We never thought people might be sympathetic to vampires. We should have, they're all over popular media. But we always assumed if the vampires went public that people would fear them, that they would run to us for help. How could we plan to be the bad guys?"

Someone was walking towards them, crunching the leaves scattered across the sidewalk beneath their feet. Calla stood up, rather than yell at her best friend. And what moral high ground did she have? She was still formulating a reply when the person stopped in front of them.

Calla didn't recognize the woman but there were teeth marks on her neck and the smell of blood clung to her. "Ms. Chase, Isolde sent me to fetch you."

Calla looked up, trying to find something to calm her. But the city's lights blotted out the stars and all that was left was a blank expanse of darkness. She took a deep breath and returned her gaze to the woman before her. "Well here I am, ready to be fetched."

"I..." The woman tugged at the bottom strands of her hair. "I think it's really brave what the hunters do. I know you might not believe that from me, but I do. And I think you'll find that Isolde is—"

"I'm sorry, I can't listen to this. Not right now."

"Of course. I'm Beatrix. If you'd follow me..." The woman was a bundle of nerves, changing her weight from foot to foot. Lisbet looked her over and red spread across her pale cheeks. She was in such a state Calla couldn't help but feel sympathy for her.

"Yes. I'll see you around, Lis."

"I love you, bestie." Lisbet stood and pulled Calla into a hug. "I'll be extra mean to Gus for you."

"I love you too. Alright, Beatrix, take me to hell."

Beatrix's face contorted into something between amusement and horror, and in the end she just nodded. For a while, she was silent, moving between people and doing a fantastic job of traversing the city's uneven sidewalk in heels, but after a few minutes her face returned to its normal color and she spoke. "You must hate this. I know I would. I mean... Well, you're being used. That's always bullshit. But, and please don't stake me for saying this, you've been raised one way. And I get it, I'm not judging..."

"Beatrix there has to be a point here." Calla pulled her jacket tight across her chest.

For the first time, Beatrix actually laughed. "Yeah, I'm just a little scared you're going to stake me. But what I'm trying to say is that they trained you to hate the vampires, and it made sense. I've read their history. But they have made an effort to be better. Plus, everything is a mess. They're afraid and you're afraid and the whole world is afraid."

"So they're kidnapping me? Come on. This is a ridiculous plan."

"They're vampires. They're dramatic. But you also haven't seen her house yet." She stopped in front of a cherry red car. Calla didn't know much about cars, but she knew expensive when she saw it.

"Are you going to blindfold me?"

"What? No." Beatrix pulled the door open. Though there was still a faint blush to her cheeks, she no longer looked like she might sink into the sidewalk.

Calla hesitated. "Where is my mother?"

"I'm not sure. You'll get to see her though. You aren't a prisoner."

The city seemed to expand in front of her. She could run. She could refuse. She could disappear into the crowd and forget she was a hunter, forget all of this. But she ducked her head and got into the car and the door shut. Moments later Beatrix was beside her in the driver's seat, then they were moving.

"I'd never stake you."

Beatrix glanced at Calla. "That's good."

They lapsed back into silence. How had this happened? Calla kept turning it over in her head as the city streets gave way to suburbia, but no matter how she looked at it she couldn't make sense of it.

Only a few hours ago she was getting stood up. Now she had to pretend to be in love with a vampire. And for what? To fool the public? And the worst part was she worried it would work.

She was charming enough, and she'd seen a mirror, she knew she was cute. Isolde was stunning, graceful, and charismatic. Despite her being the reason vampires were in the open, the public had already warmed to her. No one had found the identity of the man she had been attacking but the shock had quickly given way to awe. If she got a hunter to fall in love with her, who could really argue that vampires could fit in? That was the final hurdle, after all. Love. Not adoration. Not obsession. But love, Calla was sure, would turn the tide.

The vampires were all over the news, mostly beautiful and young, and smiling at the crowd. Then there would be some frowning hunter or Council member, explaining how they'd kept humans safe from vampires for millennia. How everything the public was hearing was only PR, and vampires were still dangerous, still volatile. Or at least it had been at first. Then it had stopped, the Council had forbidden them from making appearances, said they needed time to figure things out.

She leaned back into the leather seat and stared out of the windshield without seeing. What could Isolde really want? There had to be more to it than what she had said. But maybe there wasn't. Maybe, and Calla hated to admit it, they had the same problem. The organizations they had devoted their life to had turned on them, and they didn't know how to exist without them.

Despite her frustration with the Council, part of her hoped this would bring her back into their good graces. But could she get on board with it? Was there really a middle ground to find? If the vampires no longer fed on humans, could she accept them? Would she ever be in their presence and not feel the urge to reach for her stake, to see how they moved and figure out their weak points. Would she ever not know exactly where their no-longer-beating heart resided?

She hadn't found any answers to her questions by the time the car turned and made its way down a long driveway. They stopped in front of an enormous gate with iron bats, their wings stretched wide, attached to the front. Beatrix typed in a code, careful not to let Calla see. The gates swung open and the bats parted, granting them entrance.

They moved along a tree-lined driveway, and the largest house Calla had ever seen came into view. The outside was all dark stone that shone in the moon, reminding Calla of tombstones. A wide walkway flanked with gargoyles led up to even wider front doors inlaid with stained glass. More gargoyles, their eyes wide and sightless, guarded the windows. It was something out of a gothic horror. The monstrosity had literal turrets, spiraling up into the sky. The car came to a stop and the desire to run nearly overwhelmed Calla. She dug her fingers into the thick leather of the armrest.

This was real. She was going to live here. The air seemed colder than in the city when she opened the door. She got out and steadied herself with a hand on the car. The lights inside the house flickered, each well lit room an eye staring down at her.

"See, isn't it beautiful?" Beatrix asked.

Anywhere else Calla knew it would be, but she couldn't see it. All she could see was a prison. For all her smiles and blushes, Beatrix hadn't let her see the gate code. The Council had sold her as a political prisoner in a move she could not make sense of. No one but Lisbet had even bothered to say goodbye. Calla blinked away the tears that threatened to fall. She would not cry.

"The doors are unlocked. I'll see you soon." Beatrix smiled. "It's going to be okay, Calla. I wouldn't drive you into danger."

"No offense, but I don't know you at all and you have fang marks on your neck."

Beatrix's hand slid to her neck while red bled across her cheeks. "No, of course. But like I said... you were raised one way. But maybe there's another way, you know?"

"You aren't going to walk me in?"

Beatrix chewed her lip and Calla wondered if the shyness was real or an act, a way to get people to trust her. "No. I've got to put the car away. I really do hope you like it."

"I doubt it, but thank you." Calla watched Beatrix drive away, but couldn't get her feet to move. If she ran, what would happen? She wasn't sure she was ready to find out. What if she didn't run or go in? What if she just stood in the yard and didn't move? Would someone come out eventually or would Isolde leave her to sleep in the driveway? Part of her wanted to find out.

Instead, she finally forced herself to walk until she was standing at the front door. Up close she could see the scene in the stained glass, a woman dancing in one door, kneeling in front of a king in the other. She touched the brass door knocker but didn't knock. She pushed the door open, straightened her shoulders, and stepped through the threshold. Inside the house was illuminated by candlelight, flickering and casting shadows across the wood floors.

Her mouth went dry as she walked further inside the cavernous space. A wide staircase led upstairs but Calla did not ascend, instead she wandered to the left, through the foyer and into a large... sitting room? She had no words for the rooms of the house, each one occupied by antique furniture in pristine condition. The house was immaculate, no dust, no mess, though there was clutter, surfaces full of books and knickknacks—little figurines, daggers with polished handles, feathers and small, bleached bones.

She kept wandering, her footsteps echoing off the walls, until she came to a wide doorway, red curtains were pulled and draped on each side, giving it the appearance of a theatre stage. Calla gasped as she stepped inside a library nearly as large as the public one near her apartment.

Tall shelves, each of them crammed with titles new and ancient, stretched out so far she couldn't see the end of the room. She ran her fingers over the spines as she walked through the rows. She hadn't seen a single screen in the house, no TVs, no tablets, no phones, but at least she would be able to read.

Something moved behind Calla, and she turned to find Isolde watching her from the end of the row.

"You're free to read whatever you like. I know this is not ideal, but it's only a few months." The candlelight flickered over Isolde's face, rendering her features even sharper than usual. "Can I offer you something to eat?"

"I'd like to speak to my mother."

"From my understanding she will be free within the hour and then you can call her. Your things are in your room. If you do not wish to eat, I can show you to your room."

Calla squashed down the desire to refuse just to be obstinate. "You can send the food to my room."

"No." Isolde stepped closer. "We will eat together. We must get to know each other, Calla. And I do want you to know me. I want you to see my perspective."

"As a bloodsucker?" Calla stepped back, but a rolling ladder was behind her and she knew retreat would do her no good. "I'm good on that. I'll do what you ask, but you won't find a friend in me."

"Very well. I will show you to your room, you can freshen up, and then we will have dinner." She turned without waiting for an answer, and Calla didn't see many options besides following. Isolde led her through the rooms she had already explored and then up the stairs. Hallways spread out on each side and Calla started towards the left, inexplicably drawn to one of the rooms. There was something, a feeling, a desire. It skittered along her skin like a whisper on a breeze. She put her palm against the door.

"Leave that be. Your room is this way and you have no business in there."

"Why?" Calla wanted inside the room more than anything. What secrets did Isolde keep?

"Because," Isolde was close, too close, the curve of her fangs visible under her red lips. Her freckles a constellation on her skin. "I said you are not to enter." She smiled, and it was worse than the sneer. "Calla, we do not have to be so hostile. We could have fun." Gently, she placed her fingers on Calla's hip and tilted her head, looking up at her with wide brown eyes shrouded by thick lashes.

Calla slapped her hands away, putting space between herself and the vampire. "Whatever ideas you have, lose them."

Isolde shrugged. "You will cooperate, Calla, or I will stand by my promises and your mother will suffer. Now…" She brushed past Calla and opened a door. "Change and meet me downstairs in fifteen minutes. You reek of the city. Humans smelled so much better before automobiles."

Calla stepped inside as Isolde stepped out. Her arm brushed against Calla's, her skin was cool. Isolde pulled the door shut behind her, and Calla pressed her forehead to the wood until it hurt. Fuck. This was so beyond all of her training.

"Hello!"

Calla spun towards the voice, lifting her fists, but it was only an older woman waiting near the window. "Shit, you scared me."

"I apologize. I thought Ms. Isolde might have warned you I was here, but I suppose it slipped her mind. My name is Molly." She brushed a strand of graying, strawberry blonde hair behind her ear. "It will be lovely to have someone else in the house. Oh!" She glanced out the window while Calla willed her adrenaline to stop pumping through her body. "It looks like the rest of your things are here. In the meantime, can I help you get changed?"

Whatever she had been expecting it wasn't a servant. Was that even what this woman was? Calla knew how to keep her cool in so many situations, but nothing had prepared her for living in a vampire's mansion or having someone ask to help her get dressed—a task she had perfected before kindergarten. "I can dress myself."

"I'd be happy to help." Molly smiled and headed for the armoire. She pulled open the doors to reveal a mass of opulent dresses in varying jewel tones. Calla didn't see a single pair of pants among the whole thing. "Missus requested this one." She pulled out a slinky silk dress in pale pink.

"No way. I wear jeans." Calla couldn't help but laugh. This was ridiculous. "Is she throwing a party?"

"Oh, don't argue, dearie. It's quite a lovely dress and we'll want to get your clothes washed up for you."

Did she really smell that bad? "No." The vampires had taken enough from her. She wouldn't play dress up, especially not in private. She wasn't a doll, she was still a hunter, however blackmailed she might be. "I'm hungry and I'm going to eat and I'm doing it in my own clothes."

"Well, I don't presume that I could talk you out of it or stop you, but I think you're making a mistake. There is a brush and mirror over here."

"I look forward to seeing you around, Molly." Calla tipped an imaginary hat, bolstered by her refusal to cooperate—or maybe the day was just catching up with her. Whatever the reason she felt light on her feet, the way she usually did after a satisfying fight, as she stepped back into the hallway.

Yes, she was trapped in a vampire's house.

Yes, her way of life was probably over.

Yes, she was spinning out of control.

But at least she could annoy the ever-loving shit out of Isolde on her way to hell.

| Four |

THE hallway was empty and the smell of something delicious drifted up from the floor below. There was still time to escape, it would only take her a few minutes to get off the property and then she could be on a plane before sunrise. But the locked door seemed to call to her. The same strange pull, a sensation she could not name.

What could be in there? Something that Isolde couldn't move, though she knew Calla would be there. Her imagination ran wild, concocting all kinds of scenarios from banal to fantastical. A horde of vampires, a counterfeiting operation, gallons of blood. None of them explained what she felt. She needed to know.

But not yet. She'd get in that room. She'd find out the secret. But first Isolde had to trust her, at least a little bit, enough to leave her alone, or as alone as she could be in that house. She started down the stairs but her phone rang.

Mom

"Hello? Mom, are you okay?"

"Hey baby. I'm okay." But Delphine didn't sound okay. Her voice was hoarse and full of a sadness Calla rarely heard. "Sweetheart, you can't live with a vampire."

Calla's fingers tightened on the phone. She wanted to see her mom, to wrap her arms around her and smell her perfume. But it would have to be enough to know she was alive, she was free. "It's not so bad, mom. The house is enormous and there's a perky lady trying to dress me. I'll be okay."

"Calla..." She sighed and Calla could imagine her dragging her fingers through her hair. "Yeah, I hope so. I love you, Calla Lily."

"I love you too, mom. I should go though." She was too in the open. Though she wasn't discussing anything important, she didn't want to be overheard, and she had no doubt the vampire had ears and eyes everywhere in the house.

"Okay. I'll talk to you soon. I'm heading to the Council. I promise I'll find a way to get you out of this."

Before Calla could argue the line went dead. She dug her nails into her palms to keep from destroying something, and in this house whatever she destroyed would probably be a thousand years old. She wouldn't be surprised if she received an itemized bill at the end of her stay.

Calla went through a list in her head of all the things she'd gone through that had been worse than this, but in all of those situations—every fight, every ambush—she'd felt in control. Sometimes control would escape her for a moment, but she always knew she'd get it back. She'd trained for fighting, for how to outmaneuver a stronger enemy. She had never gone into a fight afraid.

"Fuck." She shook her head to clear it. Her thoughts were going in circles. All she had to do was eat dinner, figure out exactly what Isolde wasn't telling her, and then she'd find the control she longed for.

She continued towards the dining room, where the doors were already open. Calla wasn't sure what she'd been expecting, but it wasn't the small table set for two with Isolde smiling in front of a martini glass full of blood. But the smile fell from her face. "What are you wearing?"

"My clothes." Calla pulled out her chair and sat.

A muscle in Isolde's jaw twitched. "You will wear nicer things when we are in public."

"Maybe. Maybe not." Calla shrugged. Watching the irritation creep across the vampire's features was better than any drug. "Maybe you'll wear jeans. You own jeans, right?"

Isolde tapped her fingers on the table. Was there even going to be food? Vampires couldn't eat. Maybe they'd just sit here until the sun rose seeing who could say the most sarcastic thing until one of them broke. "What do you know of vampire history? Of where we came from?"

Or maybe things would get interesting. "Very little, as you know. I believe you killed several historians yourself. The fire, of course, was never linked to anyone." Calla smiled. "Are you about to confess your crimes to me? I'm all ears."

Isolde's nostrils flared, and she tapped a teaspoon against her glass but didn't elaborate. "What do you know about me?"

Calla leaned back in her chair, linking her fingers behind her head. "Lets see... you're way too old for me, seven hundred or so. You were some king's mistress but things didn't go so well so you fled, did a bad job at that as well, got turned and murdered your way to America. What do you know about me?"

"Well, I now know that you don't know everything about me. I know you come from a long line of vampire hunters, your bloodline being generally passed down through the maternal side. You don't know your father. You're a Council favorite, but you're hot headed and hard to control. You're beautiful, as the women in your family tend to be, which would make you the perfect person to represent the Council publicly, if only you would cooperate."

"Pretty good. How'd you get turned into a vampire?" A gilded door to the back of the room opened and a well-dressed man came in carrying a silver platter. The scene was like something out of one of the regency romances her mother loved, and if she wasn't being held prisoner Calla would have found it funny.

"I believe it's my turn to ask a question." A second man followed the first, heading for Calla, while the first sat the platter in front of Isolde and removed the lid to reveal another glass full of blood.

Calla let out a bark of laughter. "You can't seriously act like this all the time. Just be normal." The man's eyes grew wide as he laid a platter in front of Calla. Inside was a whole chicken, roasted potatoes and candied carrots. It smelled delicious. At least if she was going to be held captive she would have decent food. Before she could offer her thanks both of the servants scurried out of the room. *Servants.* The whole place was a strange mockery of elegance—timeless, brutal, and untethered to what was happening in the outside world.

"If I wanted to be normal, I would have died seven hundred years ago. To answer your question I did not choose to become a vampire, and it did not happen when I was on the run. For many years I regretted it very much, but, as I am still alive and not long ago moldered, I suppose there is a beauty to this life."

Calla pulled a leg off her chicken. Part of her wanted to pretend she didn't care what Isolde had to say, but she'd never talked to vampires before, only killed them. "So, why the change? You killed people for centuries and now you're drinking what... bunny blood?"

Isolde smiled and stood. Calla's heart skipped a beat, imagining the vampire pouncing, but she only moved her seat closer to Calla. "I would never drink bunny blood. This is donor blood, and I have drank donor blood for much longer than what has been required by the Directorate. I never *liked* the killing, except in a few cases that I don't think even you would argue with. But I was born without power, all I had was myself, my wits. So I fucked a king, but that wasn't real power. That could be taken away." She leaned closer, and once again Calla could count the freckles on her pale nose, she could smell her smoky scent. "You may not understand because you were born with power, with speed, with quick reflexes. But the rest of...we have to get by on less."

Calla skewered a carrot, pretending not to feel the myriad of things that were lighting her body on fire. "Do you think what I had was power? I was born with a target on my back. I learned to fight before I learned to read. Even if it was power, it wasn't freedom."

"Very well..." Isolde's tongue darted out, wetting her bottom lip, and Calla couldn't help but watch.

This was going to be harder than she had anticipated. Being in the same room with Isolde made every nerve in Calla's body feel exposed, what was it going to be like when they were in public? When they were touching? "If you hurt my mom, I'll do the same to you."

Isolde took a sip of blood and placed her drink down. Calla tightened her fingers around her fork but the vampire just sighed. "I don't want to hurt your mother. I want peace. There are ways for us to work together. If you weren't so hostile we could have a wonderful time."

"No. We couldn't. I don't think this is going to work, Isolde." Calla pushed her plate away. She wasn't hungry.

Isolde caught Calla's hand in her own, trapping it on the table. "Do not misunderstand this moment for either kindness or weakness. This will work, because I don't *want* to hurt your mother, but I will. You will stand by my side, and you will smile and laugh and be as malleable as the Council always wished you were. You will make people believe that even Calla Chase could find a place for vampires in her heart. You *will* find a place, however deep down in that hunter's heart you have to go. And Calla, if you don't you will never leave this place. You will not avenge your mother, you will rot in a shallow grave."

Calla wretched her hand away and stood up, sending the chair tumbling to the ground. "Fuck you."

Isolde stood, more gracefully than Calla. "What did you think? That you would come here and stake me in my sleep? Or maybe something else? That you would charm me, and I would let my guard down? I want this to work, Calla. I don't want to drag you out for events and keep you locked in a room. You are a beautiful woman, you deserve much more than that. And I don't mind putting in the effort. But I will get what I want, I always have."

"As have I."

Isolde laughed, and Calla wanted to strike her. Every muscle in her body longed for it. But not yet. "Now, there is an event in two days, a book signing—"

"I can't go. I told a woman off for putting up posters right before you called. I'm sure she'd recognize me." As much as she'd love to sabotage Isolde's plans she worried for her mother. She could sabotage Isolde, make her life more difficult, but she would always have to toe the line, never push too far. Not until her mother was free. Then there was a wooden stake with Isolde's name on it.

Isolde waved away her concerns. "We'll take care of that, I'm sure she was just some marketing intern. You will be there. This is not a hard task, there will be drinks and good company. You will wear a nice dress and look gorgeous. You'll pretend you think I hung the moon until you actually believe I did. And I know you will, because you know the consequences. Now, you should get some rest, and I'm sure you'll wake up tomorrow in a better mood. *Go.*"

But she didn't. She should but her feet wouldn't move. Calla grabbed Isolde by her chin. "You are not as frightening as you think you are."

Isolde moved with vampire speed, knocking Calla off her feet. She landed on her back with a thud that reverberated down her spine. Isolde crouched on top of her, but before she could speak Calla sprang up, her hunter training taking over and flipped Isolde onto her back. Isolde's eyes went wide, the pupils blown out, dark orbs like a starless night. Calla paused, her hand on Isolde's throat, and the vampire knocked her arm away.

"This won't end well," Calla said, pushing herself off the vampire and sitting on the floor. "Pick someone else. One of us will kill the other."

Isolde sat up, bringing her knees to her chest, and for a brief moment Calla could see the human girl behind the vampire. She had been so young, barely more than a girl. "Who else, Calla? Do you have a colleague whose mother also murdered a high-ranking vampire on tape?"

Calla pressed her palms to her eyes. "Tell me the truth. Am I a prisoner here?"

"Yes."

"Were you always like this?"

"No. My mother was beautiful and kind. I had seven brothers and sisters. I was a happy child until I was old enough for men to notice me. I was a wild girl. I wanted to live, to see the world and be something more than what I was. And I died for it.."

Calla's head hurt from the tennis match that their encounter had been. But what else was there? They were trained to hate each other and now they needed each other—forced by Isolde's hand but also Calla's mother. Neither of them were ready for the situation they had been thrust into. She sighed. "I got stood up tonight. That's how my night started, and I didn't think it would get worse."

"Are we bonding now? Are you done trying to murder me?"

"No, but I can't right now, and I don't think I'm going to be able to sleep, and I doubt you have cable."

Isolde threw her head back and laughed, her long hair brushing the ground. "I will try to be less...pushy, if you will try to squash your hunter's drive to kill me." She stood and put out her hand.

Calla took it and let the vampire pull her to her feet. "No deal. Neither of us will keep that promise. You're fucking annoying and I do want to stake you. Let's just say we won't draw blood for at least a week."

Isolde brushed off the front of her dress and straightened her sleeves. "You really should get some rest. It's late."

"Yeah. Fine." Calla nodded and headed upstairs. She went slowly, listening to her footsteps echo through the house. Her thoughts went back to the same things she had been thinking about all night. But what good was it? Did it really even matter if she hated the vampire or not? What would it change?

She pushed open the door to her room and was relieved to find no one inside. The rest of her things had been delivered and already put away but she had no energy to change. She stripped down to her underwear and got into the bed. It was annoyingly comfortable, and she sunk into the mattress.

She stared at the white ceiling and tried to make sense of what had happened to her. She was adrift, this house was not the place for her but neither was her apartment. Everything she owned had been bought by the Council. She had no skills outside of fighting, no higher education or anything to fall back on. But Calla knew how to sleep when she had things on her mind, or she would have spent months of her life not sleeping at all.

When she woke up something was different, something she couldn't quite put her finger on until she got out of bed, and inspected her surroundings. The armoire was slightly ajar, and she was almost certain it hadn't been that way when she went to bed. Or maybe she was just being paranoid. She'd earned a little paranoia though, all things considered.

Calla stretched and tried to remember exactly how the room had been the night before. Nothing else seemed different, not that she knew the room well enough to truly judge. Whatever. She hoped it was rats. It would serve Isolde right to have a bunch of rats running through her haunted mansion. Calla pulled open the door to the armoire and... yeah, she hoped goddamn termites were chewing their way through the foundation.

All of her clothes were gone. Replaced by the sort of medieval meets Victorian meets 1920s glam bullshit that Isolde usually wore. "Fuck you, Isolde, you dirty bloodsucker!" she yelled though she doubted the bloodsucker in question was close enough to hear.

Well, she had only promised not to draw blood for a week. Falling asleep last night she'd thought maybe she would try a gentler approach, hope for another glimpse of the humanity inside the vampire. But no, she was going to be the biggest pain in the ass Isolde had ever encountered. She pulled off her top as someone knocked on the door. "No."

"No?" came Molly's voice, and the door swung open. "Oh, apologies." Though she didn't look very apologetic. "Isolde was hoping you would meet her for breakfast."

"Sure thing." Calla reached for her bra, clasped it, and kicked off her pants, leaving her in underwear and pushed past Molly.

"Ms. Chase!"

Calla moved quickly, not turning around to look at the woman following her. The rugs lining most of the floor were soft on her bare feet. But the house was still a crypt, all the curtains were pulled shut and only candles lit the space, though bulbs were fitted into the chandeliers above her head.

The door to the dining room was shut and Calla pushed it open. "Morning, 'Solde. Do you have any pancakes?" She slid her underwear clad ass into the straight-backed chair.

"What is this?" Isolde looked at Calla over the top of the morning paper.

"Hmm? No pancakes, then?" Calla pretended not to know what she was talking about, determined to make Isolde as angry as she was. "So, with the whole stupid dating plan, you don't think us both being women will hurt your cause?"

"People who don't like lesbians aren't ever going to like vampires, Calla." She put down the newspaper, folding it neatly.

"So you think queer people will be vampiric allies? That's a bit presumptious."

A muscle in Isolde's jaw twitched, a small victory in Calla's mind. Even if she wasn't fuming she was irritated. "Where are your clothes?"

"Well," Calla leaned forward. "That is a fantastic question. Where *are* my clothes?"

"I am already weary of this argument, Calla." She pushed the newspaper to the side and picked up a cup of something steaming. Hot blood? *Gag.* "Your clothes are inappropriate for our—"

"My clothes are my clothes." Calla crossed her arms over her chest. "This isn't some event. This is breakfast, even if you are drinking blood in lieu of coffee. And I'm also weary of this argument, but we'll keep having it if you insist. Just going round and round."

Isolde closed her eyes for a moment, when she opened them she stared right at Calla, like she could see under her skin if she just tried hard enough. "You should have nicer clothes than what your hunter salary provided. We could go shopping."

A laugh burst from Calla's lips before she could stop it. "You want to take me shopping?" It was *something* though. She could tell Isolde was making an effort. An effort to fix a problem they shouldn't have had in the first place, but an effort all the same.

"Yes, Calla. I want to take you shopping. I prefer not to spend my whole life in this house and I doubt you want that either. So we will go out, we will try not to strike one another and we will deal with this whole thing head on." She nodded as though she had solved everything.

Calla skewered a sausage with her fork. "But what is the whole thing? Explain why the vampire Directorate is making you do this."

The room was silent, while the muscle in Isolde's jaw twitched again. When she closed her eyes, Calla wondered how long until she would open them. Finally, she did, flattening her palms on the table. "We both work for secret organizations but you were, and I mean no offense, a grunt. You did what you were told. I worked my way up, I did the telling. I made the plans for how we would come out to the humans, how we would integrate into society and then I ruined it. I was caught. I am being punished and you are being... You're a pawn, Calla. And I'm playing you, too, but I also see that you can be more. If you actually believed in what I am trying to do, we could go far together."

No words came to Calla. She wasn't a pawn. Or at least she'd never seen herself that way. She was a warrior, a fighter in a worthy cause. "I believe in the Council." But that was a lie. She had believed in them before, never once doubting them in her whole life, happy to put herself in danger to help others. "Okay, you give me my clothes back, and I'll let you take me shopping."

Isolde smiled, but it didn't reach her eyes. "We will work on your belief in the Council."

"Do you believe in the Directorate?" Calla stretched her arms above her head and rolled her shoulders, fighting back a smirk at the way Isolde's eyes trailed up her skin.

"Yes," she said without thought. "I believe in the vampires, and I believe in the work we have done. Do not speak on things you do not understand."

A moment of understanding had passed between them but it once again shattered, breaking into a million little pieces and no matter how they put it back together they were enemies. Vampire and hunter. And Calla was a prisoner, no matter how beautiful her captor.

| Five |

THOUGH the city looked as it always had, the magic of it had broken for Calla. There was no longer a world of possibilities spread before her, endless doors to open and adventures to be had. There was only the vampire at her side, the servants trailing in their wake. A nightmare that she could not wake up from.

Her mother had not called again, and Lisbet had not answered when Calla had tried to call her. She suspected the Directorate or the Council was behind it, but how could she prove it? What would proving it even do? The situation was as it ever was. There was a video of her mother murdering a vampire. Even in the best of times they tried not to get caught on tape, and now it could land her mother in jail.

"Here." Isolde stopped, pushing open the door to a shop Calla had wandered by many times but had never had the bank account to allow her to enter. She'd gotten her jeans back and had layered an old flannel over a tank top. Isolde looked like she'd just stepped off a runway styled by some quirky vintage designer. She even had a little hat, with black feathers that laid across her forehead.

There was an exquisite woman straightening the racks and she turned towards them, a wide grin spreading across her face. "Oh, darling. I'm so glad to see you." Her eyes moved over Calla and her smile cracked a bit. "Who is this?"

Isolde put an arm around Calla's waist and pulled her closer. Calla wanted to claw at her, but managed to do something close to smiling. "This is Calla. I'd love to revamp her wardrobe."

"Revamp?" Calla hissed and Isolde shot her a cloyingly sweet look. "Right. Yes, I'd love some of your... clothes." She would never admit it, but she actually did. She and Lisbet had drooled over their window displays plenty of times. Okay, maybe she'd admit it just a little. "Last month you had a dress, strappy back, off the shoulder?"

"Oh, yes. That is gone, but I think I understand what you're looking for. Wait here and I'll grab some options and get you two a private dressing area." The woman turned towards Isolde. "You have to start telling me when you're coming by. By the time you get here it's all picked over, and I hate for you to see it this way."

Isolde waved her concerns away with the arm that wasn't wrapped around Calla. "I'd never describe anything here as picked over." Her grin faded as the woman walked away and she pulled Calla closer. "Did you notice me not going for the jugular? How I'm a regular customer?"

"My girlfriend. A regular bloodsucking customer." Calla booped her on the nose. She almost laughed, but it died in her throat when a curtain to the changing rooms slid to the side and Gus stepped out in a tailored suit.

"Calla." His eyes moved to the arm around her waist and then the vampire at her side. "You actually went through with it." He looked like he'd stepped in something nasty.

"Who is he?" Isolde asked Calla, as though he wasn't there.

"I'm Gus."

Isolde kept looking at Calla.

"That's Gus," Calla said, and a little piece of her—a very little piece—loved Isolde for the cold shoulder she was giving a man who had been nothing but a thorn in her side. "Member of the council."

"Ranking member?" Isolde turned towards him, ice lacing her voice. Calla had no idea why she'd decided to hate him, but it was fun to watch Isolde toying with someone else.

Gus floundered. He was working his way up, but he was a junior member, still without votes. "You look better in person than that snuff film."

"That suit doesn't fit you," Isolde said and Gus pulled at the sleeves. "No, not the size. It is a lovely suit, but you are suited to something more plain. A t-shirt perhaps?"

Gus scoffed and turned towards Calla. "I can't believe you actually did it. I wasn't good enough, but this *thing* is?"

Before she could open her mouth, the woman who ran the shop reappeared, looking between her customers. Her smile grew wider, a customer service professional through and through. "You look fantastic, Mr. Cadieux. Right this way, Isolde." She held open the curtain, and Calla followed Isolde through it.

She nodded along as the woman, named Eliza she learned, showed her more clothes than she had in her current wardrobe and then turned to Isolde as soon as she was gone. "What was that?"

"You don't like him. Your heart rate increased."

Her heart rate increased? Isolde was monitoring her heart rate? "So you decided to pester him?"

Isolde cocked her head to the side. "Darling, why are you feigning upset over this?"

"Because, sweet cheeks..." She didn't know why. It had been funny. "Don't keep track of my heart rate, okay?"

Isolde shrugged. "Try on your clothes."

God, she was irritating. Were all vampires as annoying as Isolde? She'd spent a lot of time fighting them but very little interacting with them. She wished she had her stake. She grabbed a black dress with a low cut front and disappeared behind another curtain. The whole place was full of hanging fabric, billowing in the air conditioning.

She pulled off her clothes and slipped the dress over her head. The anger faded from her body as she turned towards the mirror. She looked incredible, even with her hair down and nothing but mascara. It fit her like a glove. She didn't bother to look at the price tag, that was Isolde's problem.

Part of her longed to be irritated that she was finally getting to try on clothes she'd dreamed about and it was all because of a vampire, but that part was overshadowed by how fucking hot she looked. She'd never gone for much style in her wardrobe, instead focusing on mobility but this was how she'd always wanted to dress. Lisbet had made fun of her for the fashion magazines that always littered her coffee table but she couldn't get enough. Women she couldn't be, women who dressed to look cute and show off their legs without worrying if their underwear would show when they staked somebody.

She didn't want Isolde to see it. Didn't want her to say how nice she looked and ruin the magic of *the* little black dress. She stuck her head out and grabbed another dress, yellow and more formal than the other.

"That would be nice for an event the Directorate is hosting next week," Isolde called after her.

49

Once she tried it on, she had to agree. It was sleek and clung to her, but still had movement when she turned. She smoothed it at her hips. This one was as low cut as the other. Eliza must have thought she had good tits. There was also a slit up the leg, leaving a lot of her exposed. She loved it. If the cameras were going to be on her—and she knew they would—let them get a good show.

Calla stepped out in the dress and Isolde moved strangely, as though she might stand up and then thought better of it. "Do I look good enough to eat?"

"Don't be crass." But Isolde's eyes dragged across Calla's body, too slowly to be anything but indecent. "You look beautiful. The public will love you."

The words slammed into her. She had always lied, never telling people who she truly was but going out with a vampire, assuring people they were safe, friendly—that was an entirely different kind of lying. Her lying had kept people safe, had been necessary to do good work. This lie was entirely selfish. She grabbed a fistful of the dress and sat down next to Isolde. "You have to really change. If I'm going to do this, you can't hurt people."

Something flashed in Isolde's brown eyes. Sadness? Irritation? Calla could never tell. "You don't know me at all, Calla." She glanced towards the opening in the curtains, towards the front of the shop where Eliza was now standing, watching them curiously. Isolde lowered her voice. "Soon I will tell you the story of why I killed that man and then we will see how you judge me."

Calla nodded but she couldn't think of anything that would endear Isolde to her. Sure she was a little funny without trying to be, and she was unbelievably gorgeous, but deep down, in all the parts that mattered, Calla saw only the beast she truly was. A killer. The woman who had kidnapped her, and no amount of fancy dresses would change that.

The curtains rustled with movement. "Stand up. Let me see it." Eliza clapped her hands together and smiled when Calla stood. "Beautiful. Do you want to keep trying things on or should I just bag up everything? I can't imagine you look bad in anything."

"We'll take it all," Isolde said.

Calla watched as Eliza retreated. Gus must have left. The shop was silent except for the beep of the cash register. It was growing late; the city moving on from shopping to activities better suited to the dark. Calla had spent the day in the library, getting lost in books and pretending she was anywhere else. But she wasn't. Everything that was happening was real. She stood up. "Help me get out of this."

Isolde followed her into the dressing room, coming up behind her to unzip the dress. Calla could have gotten out of it herself. She knew she should, that this was nothing but trouble, but she just wanted to feel something other than regret and loneliness for a moment. She missed being wanted, being important. Isolde's fingers were cold as they brushed her hair off of her shoulders.

"Where did you get so much money?" Calla whispered, watching herself and the vampire in the mirror.

"I've had centuries to grow my wealth. Plus the stock market." Isolde's breath brushed across her skin. She slowly unzipped the dress, and it fell to the floor, pooling around Calla's ankles. It was nothing she hadn't seen that morning but still her eyes snagged on Calla in the mirror.

The room had grown colder, or maybe it was Calla, so close to a vampire. Closer than she had ever been. She turned until they were face to face. She could have counted the freckles dotting Isolde's nose, the stray hairs escaping from the ridiculous feathers across her head. "I'd like somewhere to work out. Even if I'm not hunting vampires, it's still in me. I need to..."

"Let it out?" Isolde offered. "I have a training room you are welcome to use. You are not the only one with an urge to hit things sometimes." There was something anachronistic about seeing Isolde under fluorescent lights. She should be bathed in candlelight, the flame turning her blonde hair golden, her brown eyes amber. This was how vampires lured in their victims, beauty but something more, something impossible to name that drew you to them.

Calla, against all her training, wanted to ask Isolde for more of her story. How had she been turned? What had life been like when she was a girl? Instead, she stepped back and picked up her shirt off the floor. "Thanks for being mean to Gus."

"If you'll annoy a few of the Directorate, we'll call it even." Isolde bent over and picked up Calla's pants. She handed them over and her fingers brushed against Calla's knuckles.

Was it lonely being a vampire? Was she afraid of the hunters? Did she have friends? Loved ones? Had she turned anyone? But Calla could not ask those questions. Could not risk the things that answers might spark. "Oh, I'm sure I'll annoy the Directorate plenty." She pulled up her jeans, doing a ridiculous little shimmy to get into them. There was one thing she wanted to know. "Why isn't anyone answering my calls?"

From outside the dressing room, Eliza started to talk then made a little squeak when she realized no one was in the waiting area. Well, maybe that would help spread the rumors that they were lovers. But Calla kept her eyes on Isolde, looking for a tell, some sign she was lying.

Isolde only shrugged. "That is not my doing. Perhaps it is the Council."

The Council? She almost argued. It couldn't be true. But Calla couldn't argue, couldn't defend the Council. They had sold her out. They were working with vampires after teaching her to hate them her whole life. And they hadn't warned her. Had done nothing to stop what had happened. She turned away from Isolde, she couldn't look at her anymore. "What am I going to be?" she whispered towards her reflection in the mirror. The words were only for herself, but Isolde heard them all the same.

Calla braced herself for whatever she would say as Isolde stepped closer, but for a moment she didn't speak. Isolde put her hands on Calla's shoulders, brushed her thumb against her skin. "Come. We should get home." Her hands dropped. She stepped back, clearing her throat.

Like all the ones that had come before, the moment was broken, all the fragile pieces shattering on the changing room floor. Sometimes, just for seconds, Calla thought she saw a way through, a way they would get along. But there was no way. Her loneliness urged her to believe, but what she wanted to believe was not the truth. And her thoughts were a circle she could not escape. Vampires were killers. She was a hunter. They each had their places, and the vampires coming out into the public didn't change who they were. She'd seen the bodies they left behind, the grieving families they couldn't give answers to. Hers was just another life they would ruin.

Calla trailed behind Isolde on the walk home. Beatrix was following them, and she slowed her pace until she was beside her. "Why do you work for her?"

"Oh, well, what better job is there? She approached me when she started making plans for the vampires to reveal themselves. My family had witches in it, you know… before." Before the witches were gone and the magic of the world spent, except in little artifacts left behind. "So I believed in vampires." She pushed a strand of curly red hair behind her ear.

"And your family was okay with it?"

Beatrix shrugged. "Some of them were. Some of them weren't. But it's a chance to be a part of something. Can't you feel it? The way things are changing?" She whispered it, like she almost didn't believe, but Calla could see the conviction in her eyes.

They passed a bar, where TVs glowed in the windows and people drank and laughed. Calla wanted to slip in. She wanted to pick a fight, feel knuckles against flesh.

"I can show you where the liquor is." Beatrix smiled.

"Yeah, fine." Calla pulled her eyes away from the bar, back to the uneven streets of New Dunwich. There was a chill in the air, promising change. Soon the leaves would fall and then the snow. Winter had always been a busy time for Calla, when vampires had more time to be out. "Do you live close?"

"Yeah. A little walk-up on Pine, but I usually stay at the estate. Most of us do." She sighed, her eyes on Isolde's back. "I was glad it was you. I studied the Council for Isolde and you're... honestly, your whole family is incredible. You have the highest kill count of any lineage. I liked how you always did it your own way, I mean you took the jobs, of course, but some of the others..."

Calla had no idea where Beatrix was going with this. She was no different from the others—a better fighter, yes, but she did what she was told. She had always been a proper soldier. Never questioned. Sure, she went off sometimes, flew to sunny places with Lisbet. But a visionary she was not. "You've got me all wrong."

If Beatrix was right maybe things would have been easier. She wouldn't be terrified of every feeling that swelled inside of her. She wouldn't lay awake at night wishing she'd wake up a year ago, back in a life she understood. She'd always been lockstep with the Council. She'd listened without ever reaching for more. She had never longed to make the choices, never wished she had a seat in decision making. And now there was no one she could trust, but like an idiot, she was still doing their bidding. Trailing after a vampire through the night, not stalking but bantering, finding common ground she didn't want to find.

Isolde looked over her shoulder at them, her eyes narrowing. "Bea, do you have plans tonight?" Beatrix shook her head. "Good. You will stay the night. Calla could use a friend."

It was too much. "I have friends."

"Friends that do not answer your calls?" Isolde slowed her pace and a group of tourists was forced to move around her, not even noticing who they were passing. "What has she done to you? I hear her offering drinks. Why not look for comradery where you can find it? You never know when it will come in handy."

Calla curled her hands into fists to keep from lashing out. "I don't need advice from a bloodsucker." She ground her teeth. What was she doing? She felt like she had a ping-pong ball instead of a brain. "But it's your house. If you want her to stay she can stay."

"Excellent. It's settled then," Beatrix said, her pale skin flushed but she kept smiling. She looked up at Isolde from under pale lashes. "Give her time."

"I don't have time." The vampire turned on her heel and walked ahead.

Calla rushed to keep up with her, casting sharp looks at the people walking with her and they fell back. "What would the Directorate even do to you? They aren't going to stake you, are they? I mean, sure you got caught, but...what exactly are you afraid of?"

Isolde chucked and pulled the ridiculous hat off her head, somehow her hair was still perfect beneath it. "Death, Calla. The same as you. Now, leave me alone. I have things to do." She snapped her fingers and two of the servants—aids, whatever they were—rushed to her side. "Beatrix, escort her home." She turned down a side road and Calla stopped to watch her go.

There was something, a piece of the puzzle she did not know. Perhaps hidden in the room she was not allowed in, perhaps hidden deeper in Isolde's past. She looked up at the sky; the city was still too bright for stars but she could imagine them there. She sucked in a breath. She would not get her answers tonight, not with Beatrix at her side. "Drinks, then?"

"Absolutely."

The estate was spooky without Isolde in it, without the click of her heels or the flurry of staff. Calla's eyes kept straying to the staircase, wondering what was behind the locked doors. She was three whiskey sours deep and Beatrix was pleasant enough for a vampire lover. She doubted Beatrix knew Isolde's darkest secrets but she must know more about her than Calla did.

"Do you know what she has hidden upstairs? She told me I couldn't go in one room and it—" Calla clamped her mouth shut. She didn't know what the strange draw she felt was or if she was even supposed to be feeling it.

"I have an idea."

"What is it?" Calla leaned closer, clutching her drink.

Beatrix laughed, too loud and too high. She was drunker than Calla, bad at holding her liquor. "I'd never be drunk enough to tell you. They're still vampires. I don't betray their secrets."

"I'm a vampire hunter. I could keep you safe." She put her hand on Beatrix's knee.

Beatrix looked down at her hand and then up into Calla's eyes. She removed her hand, giving it a squeeze. "No offense, but look at where we are. How would you keep me safe, even if I wanted to tell you?" The tips of her ears flamed red but her gaze was steady.

Calla couldn't blame her. "Your face gives you away, you know?"

"Yeah. It sucks." She rubbed her palm against her nose. "Come on." She stood, wobbling on her feet and offered her hand to Calla, pulling her from her seat. They both almost fell back down and Calla had to lean on the wall to keep them up. She grabbed the bottle of whiskey and followed Beatrix out of the sitting room.

Beatrix didn't explain where they were going as they went up the stairs and then took a turn into a part of the house Calla had not explored yet. Judging by where they were, the library was underneath.

They came to a painting and stopped. It looked like a Renoir, soft and beautiful, but Calla didn't recognize it. "Okay?" She looked around. It was just a hallway.

Beatrix was giddy though. Calla could nearly feel the excitement coming off of her. She giggled and Calla had to admit, at least to herself, that she did like Beatrix. She was glad she was there. Her eyes were wide, and she reached out. The painting was on some kind of hinge and she pulled it forward. Beatrix pressed the open space and an entire section of the wall swung forward.

"Holy shit."

"I know." Beatrix clutched the newly revealed doorknob and pushed forward. Cold air rushed in, blowing back their hair. The whole of the estate spread before them.

"Holy shit," Calla repeated, stepping out onto the hidden balcony. She put the whiskey bottle down and turned in a circle. Lisbet would love this. "I'll deny I said it if you tell anyone, but this house is really cool." There were gargoyles on either side of the balcony and she leaned over. She could almost see the library below her, but Beatrix pulled at her shirt and they both tumbled back. "Ow."

Beatrix rubbed at her own head. "Sorry."

Away from the city, stars twinkled overhead, constellations blinking without competition from highrises. If she just looked up, Calla could almost believe she was at the start of something beautiful. She looked over at Beatrix, strands of hair falling over her pale face. "Sometimes I worry the Council was lying to me all along." She didn't know why she said it.

There was movement below them. Maybe Isolde was home. But Beatrix didn't move except to prop her head on her hand. "What if they were?"

"I don't know," she said, and pushed herself up, reaching for the bottle of whiskey and taking a long drink. "It won't mean I like vampires. But it also means... I have to figure out what I'm going to do next. I'm trapped here for now, obviously, but if I survive what's next? Who will I be? What will I do? How will I pay my bills?"

Beatrix sat up too, prying the bottle from Calla's fingers. "Calla..." Her voice trailed off. Calla wanted to know. What were the next words? When she leaned closer, Beatrix smelled like whiskey and wildflowers. And Calla was lost, adrift in an endless sea. She needed an anchor, something to attach herself to so she wouldn't get lost. She thought of the next moves, how Beatrix would taste like alcohol and how the hard balcony would feel on her bare skin.

And how Isolde would kill them. How Beatrix, besides the red on her ears, had done nothing to make Calla think she even had a chance. "Fuck." She raked her fingers through her hair. "Fine. Be my friend. I really fucking need one."

"Of course." Beatrix put her head on Calla's shoulder. And it was all fake. She was an employee of Isolde's. She was there because she was paid to be there and because she liked vampires and thought it was romantic or fantastical or whatever. But Lisbet didn't answer. Her mom wouldn't even return a text.

And it was all Calla had.

| Six |

EVERYTHING hurt. A lot. Especially her head. Calla opened her eyes, and while the sun shot daggers into her retinas, the room wasn't as bright as she expected. She'd stayed up too long with Beatrix, and now it was well past when she usually woke up. Of course it was, she was living with a vampire.

She pulled on some pajama pants and a tank top. She needed coffee. Lots of coffee. Anything to stop the pounding in her brain. She pushed open the door, half expecting Molly on the other side but she wasn't there. In fact, the house was almost silent. She could hear something far away, the faint sound of a broom against wood, but the second floor seemed deserted. She went into the hall on bare feet, careful not to make any noise.

Nothing moved. Where was Isolde? The book signing was coming up. Maybe she was busy. Beatrix must be nearby. She'd slept in a guest room, but Calla didn't hear her either.

There was nothing between her and the room where something strange resided. The something that called to her, that skittered up her skin and reminded her that magic had once been more than vampires and a few healing potions. That witches had once been feared, revered. That maybe, just maybe it was all possible again.

Calla's heart pounded. This was her chance. On tiptoes, she went back into her room and grabbed a bobby pin. She wanted something sturdier but there was no time to search for it. Someone could show up any moment. She tucked the pin into the mess of hair on her head and went back into the hallway.

She was going to get caught. She was going to get drained of all her blood, and her mother was going to pay the price for her bad decisions. Still, she moved forward until she was standing in front of the door. She paused, expecting someone to jump out and stop her. Nothing moved.

The only thing between her and whatever was inside was a simple lock. She kneeled down in front of the door, knees pressing into the wood. She slid the pin out of her hair and into the lock. It only took a moment before it clicked open.

Had Isolde really trusted her not to look? Had she thought a locked door would keep Calla out? She took a deep breath, turned the handle and pushed the door open. With a final glance at the hallway, she slipped inside the room and pulled the door closed behind her.

The room was as still as a tomb and dust motes floated through the air, caught in slats of sunlight from the windows. Most of the furniture was covered with white sheets, a room haunted by angular, squat ghosts. But in the middle of the room was an ancient hand carved table and in the middle was an hourglass, giving off the strange hum, drawing all of Calla's attention. She moved forward on shaky feet, her hands clasped behind her back.

As she got closer, the hourglass seemed to feel her presence. The humming grew, it started to glow, so faint she thought she was imagining it. Most of the dark sand was in the bottom, only a smattering remained on top.

No. Not sand.

Blood.

Drops of blood that defied gravity, hovering in the hourglass, not yet falling but threatening to. How long had it been counting down, how long until another drop fell? And what did it count down to? What happened when the last drop fell? The magic running across her skin grew thick, turning oily, into something more like fear. She wanted to reach out and brush her fingers against the glass but didn't dare. This was a magical artifact. Something old and enchanted. It would be worth a fortune. Why was Isolde hiding it?

Maybe it was just for the price or the novelty of it. Maybe it would run out and nothing would happen except that someone would need to turn it over again. But Calla didn't think so. The house was strewn with timeless, priceless objects. There was a reason this one was here.

She leaned closer, nearly pressing her nose to the glass, but couldn't make sense of it. There was so much blood on the bottom, but it didn't pool. She could have counted each drop. And it was huge, both sides almost as big as her head.

"Calla!"

She spun around. Isolde was fuming. Her sharp teeth were bared, her pupils blown wide. Calla's instincts took over. She lunged for the vampire, catching her arm and twisting it behind her back. She wrapped her other arm around her waist, pulling her close.

Isolde threw weight backwards, knocking Calla to the ground. She tried to jump up, but Isolde was on top of her, straddling her chest. "You said you wouldn't attack me for at least a week."

"I said I wouldn't draw blood." Calla freed her arm and reached up, grabbing Isolde by the throat. Her fingers dug into the vampire's flesh. She could feel the bones and muscles beneath her skin, knew the ones she would need to snap to give her time to drive a stake into Isolde's heart.

Isolde fisted a handful of her hair, yanking her head back. She leaned close, her lips at Calla's ear. She smelled of smoke and wine. "Darling, you are the one being naughty."

"Fine." Calla sighed. "I'm done." Isolde loosened her grip on Calla's hair, and Calla let her hand fall from Isolde's neck to her waist. "I'll remember this for the book signing, though. Tell them you like it rough."

The vampire was still so close, her breath moving the hair at Calla's neck, her body pressing her into the floor. "You are the one beneath *me*, Calla."

"And you're the one not moving, Fangs." Calla gripped Isolde's hip before letting her go. Isolde moved off of her. Why was she always on the ground in this goddamn house?

"I dislike that nickname." Isolde got to her feet and Calla did the same.

"Too bad. What's with the hourglass?" Isolde started to reply but Calla cut her off. "And no bullshit."

"You fight well, you know."

"And no changing the subject." Calla had half a mind to boop her nose again just to make her mad. Part of her wanted to see exactly how angry she could make the vampire. "Unless it's showing me your training room because after that I'm itching for a fight."

"Perfect. We will talk and walk." Isolde briefly glanced at the hourglass, and when she looked back Calla could have sworn it was embarrassment that swept over her face, but Calla blinked and the look was gone.

"Want to get me out of this room, huh?" Calla felt a bit like the family pet, following Isolde from room to room. She was also worried she'd never memorize the layout of this place and end up lost in some dark dungeon and starve to death. As though confirming her suspicions, Isolde took a turn and started heading down a staircase she didn't even know was there. Seriously, how big was the house?

Luckily the staircases ended in a basement and not a dungeon. And it was incredible. There was everything Calla could hope for in a training space. Punching bags, dummies, weights, benches, even a box of stakes which she wasn't going to ask about. She turned towards Isolde to compliment her. The vampire was leaning against the doorframe, her eyes dark and heavy, and all Calla could think of was Isolde's weight against her chest.

"Okay." She walked over to a kettlebell and lifted it. "Spill the beans. Why do you have an enchanted hourglass? I know you're all fancy, but you aren't showing it off so it has to be some spooky shit." She could see in the way Isolde's eyebrows pushed together that the vampire hated the way Calla talked. It warmed her heart. Anything to annoy a vampire.

"Calla, if I'm going to tell you this I'm going to need you to pretend you're actually my girlfriend or that you actually care, at least a little, about me because I was not supposed to let you see that. I wasn't even supposed to have it at my house."

Calla put the kettlebell down. "First, tell me why you killed that man. Endear yourself to me."

Isolde ran her hands through her hair then pressed her fingertips against her lips. It was the most ruffled Calla had ever seen her. She walked further into the training room. "Because he hurt someone who I cared about very much. He left her alive, but he destroyed her, and then she kept destroying herself until she was gone. Before him she was like the sun and he plucked her from the sky. He was a rapist and a murderer and he didn't deserve to live. It took years to track him down but I did it, with Directorate resources and money, I did it. And yes, I drank his blood, because I am a vampire. And... I got caught. It was too public, I wasn't thinking. I was still furious."

Calla nodded, swallowing a lump in her throat. Isolde was a bloodsucker, but there was pain on her face, and Calla was forcing her to spill her secrets. Worst of all she believed her.

At least this once.

There was a noise from above. Isolde looked up and pushed the door shut. She pressed her palms to the wood. "I'm going to tell you the truth because if my plan is going to work then there has to be something between us. So I'm doing this. I'm being vulnerable."

Vulnerable. Not a word she had ever associated with vampires. Another piece of the puzzle that made up Calla fell away. All her life she'd been told that vampires were monsters, killers in human skin. And she'd eaten it up. "Okay." She nodded, unsure why she was making a deal with a vampire.

"Are you familiar with witches?"

"Yes. I'm not an idiot." There was the Isolde Calla knew, and... well, she didn't love her, that was for sure, but she felt better when Isolde was treating her like a dumbass. She knew how to handle that. Calla rattled off what she knew. "Witches were real, they did magic. We can see it in their artifacts and simple spells, but all but the barest magic is gone, and no one is quite sure why. Is that good enough? Do I pass the test?"

Isolde paced the training room. The rubbery floor muffled the click of her heels. "Witches created vampires. I don't know the why or the how. It all happened well before my time. But my sire was turned by the first. I did not know him well but later another he had created—before me—found me, and..." She stopped, eyes wide. "I can't. Calla, they will put me in the sun."

"What?" Put her in the sun? For having a witch artifact?

"I shouldn't have had it here." Isolde sat down on a workout bench, and despite the severity of their conversation, Calla was struck with an image of her in spandex workout gear lifting weights. She nearly smiled except the horrified expression on Isolde's face stopped her.

Focus, Calla. "Well, why'd you let me go poking around if it was that serious?"

"I don't know. I... I couldn't let it go. It was mine. My mission. And I just keep trying and..." She put her head in her hands.

Calla sat on the bench beside Isolde, and goddamnit, Isolde's plan was working because sympathy coursed through her. "Okay, back up. Explain. You're in it now, might as well get it off your chest." And there she was, sitting on a bench in a training room, rubbing the back of a seven hundred year old vampire wearing some sort of vintage couture and Louboutins.

"You know most of the curse, the sun, the blood, all that, but there is another part and none of the hunters know it. But..." Isolde took a deep breath, her brown eyes fluttering shut. "I think you'll understand me better if I tell you. And we're supposed to be bringing the humans and vampires together, right?"

Calla wasn't sure she wanted to hear this. Wasn't sure she wanted to be in the middle of whatever it was. She didn't trust Isolde or any of the vampires. A few days ago she would have jumped at learning a secret that made them vulnerable, but now? It would be a millstone around her neck.

Isolde kept talking. The words slipped from her mouth, as though she had rehearsed saying them again and again but had never had an audience. "The hourglass is exactly as it seems, it is a timer made with the first vampire. It was meant to curb the cruelty that came with immortality. We had a hundred years—a lifetime—to reveal ourselves to humans and find a way to live with them. Or at least this is what I have been told. The hourglass was passed down from vampire to vampire until it came to me. When I was young, I regarded it as a cruel curse, to dangle immortal life before someone and take it away on an impossible task. Now I understand it, I see the sense of it in our cruelty and capriciousness. We were never meant to live forever like this, but we are afraid to die, afraid to change."

"But it has been more than a hundred years." Calla gripped the edge of the bench. The Council had never heard a whisper of this.

"Yes. Whoever created it did not anticipate just how far we would go to keep being cruel. Instead of integrating, we found witches and forced them to give us more time. But the witches disappeared. Our time has slipped away and I—we have until the last drop of blood falls and then we are no more."

The ping-pong in Calla's head had become a full on tennis match. She walked to one of the weights and picked it up. Put it down. "Why would you tell me this? What the fuck am I supposed to do with this information? I'm a vampire hunter, Isolde. I'm a fucking vampire hunter!"

Isolde started to move towards Calla and then stopped. "Because you saw the hourglass."

"Then lie! You should have never let me see it." Calla paced the floor. All she had to do was stall and all of this would be over. A little time and vampires would be gone—if Isolde was telling the truth.

"You broke in."

"Yeah, because you're keeping me prisoner. And for what? This crazy plan? Why can't I be at my house? Why would you trap me in here with some insane vampire secret I've never heard of?" All of it had to be a lie. But Calla couldn't make sense of it. What could she gain? What reason could she have for doing all of this if nothing was on the line? She'd taken an enormous risk by bringing Calla into her house. Was she telling the truth?

"Because... because if you weren't here you wouldn't go through with it. I've watched you. You are headstrong. You'd work with your mother and you'd figure something out and you wouldn't help me. You would have found an escape."

Calla pressed her palms to her eyes until her vision went blurry. "This is fucked up. This is all so fucked up."

"I thought if you knew—"

"If I knew? You had a hundred years to come to terms with the fact that you're dying. It's more than most have. That's real fucking rich, Isolde. And what is all this? Did you really think acting vulnerable would work? That this sad act would work on me? I'm a vampire hunter."

Her face changed, all the emotion draining from it. "I do not want to die."

"Who does?" Calla turned and slammed her fist into a punching bag. It reverberated up her arm. The truth was too heavy. She was a vampire hunter, and she had a chance to rid the world of vampires but it would mean losing her mom. Or would it? If the vampires were gone, maybe she could get away.

Calla looked at Isolde. She'd never let that happen. If Isolde realized she was going to die Calla knew she'd take her mother with her. There would be a price on their head until the moment the vampires were gone, and Calla didn't know how much longer that would be. Months? Years?

"You will still cooperate and you will tell no one about this." The mask had fallen back into place over Isolde's face, all emotion and vulnerability washed away, like words in the sand.

"If it's even true." For all Calla knew the thing counted down the seasons or the next equinox. She'd be giving up her mother's life and the vampires would still walk the earth. She needed to know the truth.

Isolde shrugged. "I know you can hurt me, but I have ways to make you hurt too, Calla Chase."

"Ditto." She steadied the still swinging punching bag. "I wish you had never told me all that shit."

"You... are not as terrible as I thought you might be. You had a right to know the truth." Isolde smoothed her dress. "Feel free to use the room. Don't forget about the book signing."

Calla watched her go then turned back to the punching bag, letting out her frustration on the leather until her knuckles were bleeding.

When she was finished, she still had no idea if Isolde was telling the truth nor why she would lie about such a strange thing. She needed a plan, but she didn't even have the barest whisper of one. No way forward looked better than any other.

Just get through the book signing. It was one event. She could do one event and maybe figure out why Lisbet and her mother weren't taking her calls. Her whole life she'd acted fast, but this wasn't the time for it. She needed to know what was true and what was lies before she did anything rash.

| Seven |

THE sun was beginning to set when Molly found Calla in the library, curled up in an armchair. Calla had spent the entire afternoon trying to figure things out before she realized that would never happen until she cleared her head. She'd been surprised to see what an enormous collection of romance books Isolde had tucked away in the back of the library—some of them absolutely smutty.

"We need to get you ready for the event," Molly said, looking her over. "Would you consider wearing gloves to cover your hands?"

Calla looked down at her scabbed knuckles. It could be worse, hunters healed fast. "Gloves seem a bit much for a book signing. And I was thinking of wearing the black dress I got the other day. It would look weird with gloves.

"You'll look lovely in it." Molly took her book and put it back on the shelf before leading Calla with a hand on her back. "I do wish you'd worn the boxing gloves. But you're a hunter. I suppose it won't be too out of place. You're a beautiful girl, Calla. You'll photograph well."

"Thank you?" She wasn't sure how to respond, but she liked Molly. She was kind and even-tempered and never seemed to pick sides though Calla wouldn't be surprised if she was reporting back to Isolde. She signed Molly's paychecks, after all. "Hey." She paused at the door to her room. "Where does Isolde get her blood? Does she have donors like... here? On site?" She hadn't seen teeth marks on Beatrix since her first day at the estate and those could have come from an entirely different vampire. She had no idea what Beatrix did in her spare time.

Molly chuckled, making the hair brushing her shoulders shake. "Generally, no. She has blood in the kitchens that gets brought in from ethical sources." She urged Calla forward until she had her in her room.

"And do you think it's fair that they get to live so long? I mean the rest of us don't get centuries to live."

Molly made her way over to the armoire. "Life isn't fair. Personally, I wouldn't want it. I love the sun. It's too much to give up. Wouldn't you miss desserts?"

Calla pulled her clothes off, still not used to being dressed by someone but at least it was Molly. "Yeah. And hamburgers." She took the dress Molly held out and pulled it over her head. She still looked as good in it as she had at the store. "Leather jacket, please."

"Calla..."

"I know, I know. But she wants the world to believe she's dating a hunter so..." She saved Molly the heartbreak and got it herself. "Speaking of... She just let you in on her plan? Isn't she worried you'll spill the beans?"

"To who? My husband. He wouldn't care, he works in the guardhouse. And besides, she pays well. Very well." Molly picked up a brush. "Sit." Calla obeyed. "Now, I don't know exactly what you know, so I won't be spilling too much, but I think you should give her a chance. She wants to protect the people she loves. You love your mother, look at all you've done for her. Do you think Isolde is heartless? Plus..." Molly's gaze moved beyond the vanity mirror, going somewhere far away.

Desperately Calla wanted to know what came at the end of the sentence, but she didn't enjoy poking at Molly like she did with Isolde, so she let it drop. The woman could tell her whatever it was on her own time. "Is Beatrix coming?"

"I believe she is. Listen." Molly stopped what she was doing and kneeled down next to Calla. "I'm not going to tell you to go along with all of this blindly. You are old enough to make your own choices, but, I sincerely hope, you are also asking yourself what lies the Council told you. You say you are a hunter but I think you are a protector. Look at what you are doing to keep people safe. Not because it is a mission but because of love. So whatever you do, do it by your own choices, Calla."

Calla could not look into her eyes, so she stared at a spot beyond Molly's shoulder. "I just want to talk to my mom."

"I will look into that for you. A girl needs her mother. For what it's worth I don't think that is Isolde's doing but I will not swear to it. Now, scoot a little so I can do your makeup."

Calla stood at the front door feeling silly. She had no idea what she was supposed to be doing, and the flurry of Isolde's employees wasn't so much as bothering to look at her, so she went outside.

"Cheerio, old chap." She patted one of the gargoyles on its shoulder. Outside the crickets were chirping and stars were shining. They weren't far from the city, but far enough that the world felt peaceful if she pretended she was somewhere else.

Get through tonight.

That's all she had to do. She would see what she could learn, manage not to barf while she pretended she was dating a vampire, and then make a plan. A plan that should probably involve trying to get back into Isolde's good graces if she wanted to get anywhere. It was just hard to hold her temper in check. She'd never been good at it, and she'd never even tried with a vampire. But the world was changing, and it was becoming increasingly obvious Calla had to change too if she was going to be a part of it.

The treeline at the edge of the property was fluttering with movement. Hundreds of bats flew through the night, their dark shapes moving amongst the branches and over the treetops. Calla stepped off the porch. She took a few steps away from the house, the furthest she'd been by herself. As she moved from the stone path onto the lawn her heels sunk into the soil.

She wanted to walk further, to see if there were any paths through the woods, but she stayed where she was, watching the bats. She'd always loved the night, as a hunter she'd spent a lot of time in it. Even humans changed in the night, inhibitions lowered, laughter coming more easily. At night a person could shrug off their responsibilities and pretend they were someone else.

"There you are," Isolde said and Calla turned towards her voice. She looked incredible. Her dress was sleek and red, hugging every curve. It was the most modern thing Calla had seen her wear. She'd forgone a hat and instead her hair was in thick curls, pinned away from her face with pearls.

"You look nice," Calla said walking back towards the house. She still itched for a stake every time she looked at Isolde, but she was gorgeous. People would easily believe someone could fall in love with her even if they shouldn't. Their relationship wouldn't be a hard sell.

"I am sorry for yesterday. I hope we can still find common ground." Isolde moved down the steps. "I have heard some of the Council will be there tonight. Perhaps you will see your friends."

It was an olive branch, and Calla took it because tonight she didn't feel like fighting. "You should tell me about your book on the way over. If I was your girlfriend, I would have read it."

"Maybe one day you will. Don't worry, I had a ghostwriter, so it's actually quite good." They both stepped back onto the porch as Isolde's car pulled up.

The driver stepped out and pulled the door open as another car pulled up behind it and Beatrix came onto the porch. Her outfit was closer to Calla's—a little black dress, nude heels and a cardigan. "See you soon."

"Yeah." Calla got into the car and Isolde slid in beside her. She wanted to be mad, she *was* mad, but she had agreed to do this so she tried to shove those feelings down. The Council would be there, she could find someone to answer her questions. She looked over Isolde. Why did she have to be so hot? If she wasn't a vampire, Calla would have been thrilled to take her on a date. She'd focus on that. A pretty woman, an open bar.

And while Isolde was her captor, she was captive too. Calla still didn't believe her story about the hourglass, but her fear that the Directorate would burn her was real. She knew what the fear of death looked like on a vampire, she'd seen it a hundred times. And she had a feeling Isolde's story about why she'd killed that man was real as well. After the shock of her confession had worn off, Calla had been left with a person. A vampire yes, but also a person with her own motivations.

And not the demon she had been taught to fear. Not exactly. Something close but also something close to her. And it was all so confusing she wanted to jump out of the car. She didn't want to feel or think any of the things going on in her head. Anger and sympathy fought for dominance every waking moment. She wished she could get into the Council, sneak into the archives they never let her see. Molly was right, she had believed everything they'd ever told her. Calla needed to know if they had believed it as well. Had they been feeding her falsehoods or had they simply passed on lies they had been told for generations?

But even if she got in, the Council had never given her the answers she'd wanted. When she was sixteen, she'd walked into a meeting and asked why they had strength and agility and fast healing. Why were the hunters made the way they were? Had they been created at the same time as vampires or had they existed before and put their powers to good use?

They'd told her to leave. And she'd done it. Her strength had never extended to the Council. She'd never fought them. She hadn't been raised to. Had her mother known? She couldn't believe she had.

She was pulled out of her thoughts by Isolde talking about her book. She told Calla about her time in aristocracy, the way her father had tried to basically sell her so she'd slept with a king to get herself out of it. How poorly that had gone when the king's wife had found out. How the king had found her bleeding out and brought her to a vampire and then could not look at her again. How the vampire had begged for a place for her in Court and the king had banished her anyway.

"Wait," Calla said. "Is this true? It's kind of... vague."

"Yes, well, it is still my life, and I have hidden it for a very long time. I would prefer to keep people from digging into some of the more enticing details, but it is true."

"So what did you do after? When you were on the run?"

Isolde chuckled. "Scammed many men to stay alive. That was before I knew any other vampires besides my maker. I had hoped my sire might follow, might show up one day, but he did not, though another of his making did, eventually. I had not even known my sire was anything other than human before he turned me. Some vampires come into it fully aware, they are embraced by the community. I was a woman in a very bad position with no knowledge of who or what I was. Finding the Directorate was... it was incredible. I had a home. And I worked my way up through the ranks. And this part is not in the books, but that is why what I did was regarded so poorly. I have lost my power, my favor with other vampires. It can not end this way."

Calla chewed her lip. Sometimes, in moments like this, she didn't feel like she was drowning. And sometimes that was worse, waiting for the next bad thing to happen. Isolde probably thought the same thing, never knowing what Calla would pull next. Part of her wanted to be disagreeable now, but Molly's words kept ringing in her ears. Whatever she did, she needed to—for the first time in her life—do it for herself.

They pulled off the interstate and headed into the city. Some emotion built in Calla's gut but she couldn't tell if it was anticipation or fear.

"What do you know about the Council?" she asked.

"Not much, honestly. We know they train the hunters. We know they want to kill vampires. We knew where most of their headquarters were but it always seemed like a bad idea to try anything." Calla made a noise and Isolde raised an eyebrow. "We knew they talked as though we were demons."

"You drink blood." Calla pointed out.

"Yes, well, I have little choice in that and I've killed far less than I've had to, which I believe is more than you can say."

Calla shrugged. "Fair enough. But isn't it worse if you aren't demons? I mean, if you're a demon then you have an excuse. If you're just killing humans—"

"To live?" Isolde interrupted. "You think I'd prefer to be a demon? You think that's the more morally sound choice? You truly have no idea of what you speak. You have no idea what it feels like to be a new vampire."

Calla chewed her lip, mulling over her next words. She had a lot to say—she always had a lot to say. Naomi had hated the way she talked back during training. But now was not the time to argue. "Okay, maybe we should talk about something else."

"Yes. I think tonight we do not pretend we are lovers. It will be too soon. The humans are not fools. We are simply friends... maybe our hands touch, maybe we laugh too much—"

"Yes, I know how to flirt. So we're just gal pals. Roomies. Sapphic sleepover pals." Calla leaned back as far as she could in the leather seats of the car.

"Does the sound of your own voice bring you some sort of joy?"

"Do you ever trip on things with your nose up in the air like that?"

"So, yes then." Isolde pulled out a bronze compact and checked her reflection. "Hate fucking, that's a thing humans say, right?" She fixed a curl.

Calla choked so badly she had to sit up. She was saved from having to think of a response by the car pulling into a parking lot. "Well, here's to selling my soul to the devil." She pushed the door open and got out. The venue wasn't crowded yet, which she was thankful for, but the lot was already half full. Calla walked around the car and pulled Isolde's door open before the driver could. "Darling..." She offered Isolde her arm.

"Stop." Isolde stood, ignoring Calla and nodded towards the bookstore. It was one of the largest in New Dunwich that wasn't a chain. Calla had spent many afternoons exploring the aisles with a chai tea. She slowed her pace, looking it over. Would it ever offer solace again after this night? After walking in and lying to everyone in the store?

Sometimes arguing with Isolde was fun. Isolde was the first vampire she'd ever had a relationship with, however strained. But she knew this part wouldn't be fun. This was betraying who she was. She wanted her mother, wanted to be wrapped in her arms, smelling her perfume.

The bookstore was done up nicely, with twinkling lights at the entrance and large posters with Isolde's face. The same poster she'd pulled down only days ago, though now it seemed like a lifetime. She followed her inside, unsure of what she was supposed to do. Before she could contemplate further, Beatrix was at her side, guiding her by the elbow to the empty space beside a podium. "You're doing great."

"I just walked in. I've always been able to walk," Calla hissed.

"Yeah, you actually look like you're going to throw up. I was just trying to calm your nerves." Beatrix smiled and leaned in. "You're not as intimidating as I worried you might be."

"Great." Calla ran her fingers over a stack of Isolde's books. "Soft is definitely the vibe I'm going for."

"Oh, I'm sure you're very spooky to everyone else."

"Why am I really standing over here?" Calla watched as a woman she recognized as one of the shop owners walked over to Isolde. How did people not care? How were they not terrified to host a vampire event in their place of business? Humans were so fucking dumb.

Beatrix cleared her throat and looked at the floor, but the more time she spent with her the more Calla was sure the nervous thing was mostly an act. A facade to get people's guard down. She might turn red easily, but she was tougher than she seemed. "I'd rather not say."

"And I'd rather not be here, yet here I stand."

"I think it's better we wait until after the reading to let people start to question you. They should hear Isolde first," Beatrix said.

It was a lie. Calla was sure of it, but everyone was smiling and laughing and downing champagne. Everyone besides Calla was there because they wanted to be. So she did as she was told and waited. It wasn't like she wanted to speak anyway.

| Eight |

A STEADY stream of people made their way through the shop doors. Calla watched them, but none of their eyes lingered on her. They were all here for Isolde. Would she have come to one of these on her own at some point? Would curiosity have eventually got the best of her?

The lights flickered, and the store grew silent. All eyes turned towards the podium. Isolde looked beautiful, timeless and perfect, as she opened her book. No one broke the silence. Isolde smiled, wider than Calla had ever seen, before she cleared her throat and began to read.

Calla scanned the crowd, looking for the woman she had screamed at when she pulled down the poster. Was she here? Honestly, Calla wasn't sure. She barely remembered her face, she could be one of several women at the event. None of their eyes hung on Calla. Had Isolde's staff told her some elaborate lie, or did the fact that Calla's hair was done and she had on more makeup than she'd ever worn disguise her? Maybe she wasn't even at the reading, maybe she really was just some marketing intern who put up posters so her boss wouldn't have to.

Calla listened to Isolde reading about her time at Court. It was all beautiful and lyrical and just as vague as the story in the car. She wondered how much of it was true. Certainly not all of it. If she had to guess, Isolde had fabricated enough details to make herself untraceable. People would still try though.

She didn't realize she had been staring at Isolde until the vampire stopped talking and glanced at her. Isolde's smile changed as they locked eyes, soft and sweet. Calla knew she should smile back, but she wasn't a great actress. So she winked. She could manage that. But everyone was looking at her, her cheeks grew hot and she looked away.

And the world seemed to wobble beneath her feet. There was Lisbet, standing at the back of the crowd, her brown eyes boring into Calla. It was only years of hunter's training that kept her from lurching forward, from pushing her way through the crowd and to her best friend. To safety.

The minutes stretched, each one lasting an eternity. She needed to talk to Lisbet, needed to know why no one was answering her calls. Why she couldn't get in touch with her mother. She massaged her bruised and scabbed knuckles.

The crowd clapped. It was over. Calla waited a moment. Another. Until people were mingling. Isolde moved off the stage. Calla knew she couldn't look too eager, didn't want to draw Isolde's attention, so she brushed by the vampire, offering her a smile. Isolde smiled back, still beaming with the adrenaline of the stage, and if it was anyone else, another moment, Calla might have believed she was happy to see her.

But there was no time to even think about that. She brushed her fingers on the small of Isolde's back, enough to hopefully satisfy whatever she was supposed to do tonight, and then she pressed through the crowd, scanning faces until Lisbet was in front of her.

Lisbet threw her arms around Calla's neck. "God, I missed you." She pulled back and looked her over. "Are you okay?"

"As well as I can be. Why is no one answering the phone?"

Lisbet looked around, her eyes wide. She motioned her head towards an empty aisle and Calla followed, her heart pounding. Visions of her mother flew through her mind. Lisbet stopped in front of a collection of travel books. "Calla..."

"Lisbet, what?" They were hunters. They'd fought side by side and she'd never seen Lisbet look so unnerved.

"Your mother is in the Council's custody." She lowered her voice until it was barely a whisper. "There is a break in the Council. Those that want to accept the vampires, who are tired of fighting and those that want to destroy them. They're coming in from other headquarters, everyone is furious. Gus is leading those out for vampire blood. Naomi leads the others, and they have taken your mother."

Calla was dizzy. She took a step back until her back was against the bookshelf. All of this for nothing. Her own people had betrayed her. "Why would Naomi do that?"

"I'm not entirely sure, but as far as I can tell the vampires are like the hunters—broken over this. Isolde made her deal with you, but others are still upset, think your mother should pay. I don't think Naomi means her harm, she's only being detained until everything has been worked out."

"I have to get her out."

"No," Lisbet said. "While Gus supports freeing your mother, he makes no moves because he is furious with you. He believes you should have taken a stand. You are in more danger than you have ever been. Some of the Council wants to capture you, to *kill* you even, to make a point."

She heard the words but she could barely understand them. She had never seen eye to eye with Gus but he wanted her dead? They'd grown up together. He'd asked her out at least a dozen times, and now he wanted to *kill* her. She needed to sit down. "What should I do?"

Lisbet glanced towards the end of the aisle and shook her head. "I don't know, Calla. I never thought I'd say this, but stay near the vampire for now. Stay alive. I'm going to figure out more, and I'll let you know when I can." She swooped in, planting a kiss on Calla's cheek. "I love you."

Before Calla could respond Lisbet was rushing away. She wanted to reach out, to call out, to stop her. But she didn't. Instead, she stood in the empty aisle, replaying Lisbet's words over and over in her head.

"Calla?" Beatrix peered around the corner. "What are you—Are you okay?"

Blinking back tears, Calla shook her head. "No. I don't think I am. I just... Can I please leave?" There was a desperate pleading in her voice that she hated to hear, but she didn't know how to dispel it, how to be the person she had been only months ago.

"Yeah. Come on." Beatrix wrapped her arm around Calla's shoulder. "We'll just let Isolde know." She rubbed Calla's shoulder as they walked, sneaking glances at her. No one had ever looked at Calla like that before, like she was a small thing, hurt and in need of help.

She was glad there had been no official introduction yet, that she could slip through the crowd relatively unseen. They left the rows of books and she steadied her shoulders and moved back into the crowd. She could fall apart later, but she had no idea who might be in the bookstore, who might lurk in the shadows watching her.

That thought kicked her hunter instincts back on. She glanced at the door, into the corners of the shop. She was busy taking stock of the familiar faces in the crowd when an even more familiar face appeared in front of her.

"What is going on?" There was no malice in Isolde's voice, but her eyes narrowed. "You disappeared."

"Sorry," Calla said. *Stay by the vampire.* Was this really what her life had come to? She sighed. "I have a lot to tell you." Because why the hell not? If there was no Council then was she even a hunter? Or was she the hunted?

"Me?" The surprise was obvious for only a second on Isolde's face before she composed herself. "Okay, later. Come, have a glass of champagne."

"Isolde..."

"Calla." She tapped her foot on the floor, but there was a plush rug beneath her and the effect was diminished. She replaced Beatrix's arm with her own. "You can go."

"I... I... She..." Beatrix stammered, her cheeks turning pink.

"Is there some danger I am unaware of?" Isolde's pointed teeth flashed in warning.

"Something frightened her." Beatrix choked out.

Isolde stiffened beside Calla. This was a fucking disaster. Calla swallowed. Okay, so Gus wanted her dead. Well, she'd wanted to strangle him plenty of times, perhaps she'd get her chance. She took a deep breath through her nose.

If Lisbet had been here, then someone was certainly watching. She'd give them a show. Let them come for her. Gus worked for the Council, but he wasn't a trained hunter. And even if he had hunters on his side, Calla was the best. She was trained, and she was a fighter. They wanted her afraid, and though part of her was, she would not let them know. She would rather the entire Council think she was fucking a vampire than show them her fear.

"At least you aren't a liar," she mumbled, then looked towards Beatrix. "I'm fine. I got some upsetting news and needed a moment, but I'm fine."

There was work to be done, and Calla was at her best when she had a task. She let Isolde lead her into the crowd, with her mind on other things. Isolde had a video of her mother committing a murder, but she had let her go. Naomi had trapped her mother. Gus was out for Calla's blood. That made Isolde the closest thing she had to an ally.

But was she? Could she trust Isolde not to betray her? At the minimum, they had a common enemy—Gus. Calla needed to get in touch with Naomi. Was it just as Lisbet had said or had her mother done something else? Had she threatened to attack another vampire? Something made Naomi think she was dangerous or in danger. Calla suspected the first. If she could get her mother out of custody, figure out what the fuck was going on, then maybe she could also get Naomi's faction on her side.

But was she really going to align herself with the side that wanted to build a future with vampires? Calla realized Isolde was looking at her. She'd said something. Calla smiled. "What?" There were people around. Hopefully, they hadn't introduced themselves because Calla hadn't been paying attention.

"Did you like the reading?" a woman asked again.

"Of course. Sorry, I'm so scattered brained, but yes, it was absolutely amazing. What a life she led." Calla bumped her hip against Isolde's.

"How do you know her?" the woman asked.

Shit. She wasn't ready for this. Well, she'd had a terrible evening, why not spice it up. "Actually, I was a hunter." The woman made a noise and Calla looked up at Isolde. There were so many jokes to make, ways to make Isolde turn red, either with embarrassment or frustration. But it was the truth that slipped out of her mouth. "It turns out we'd both been lied to."

Something inside Calla cracked, but she didn't let herself crumble. The truth had been building inside her for days. Whatever she believed about vampires, about Isolde, about the Council, they had lied to her.

What else didn't she know?

Isolde recovered quickly. "It's the beauty of being out in the world. Being able to tell my truth, to change any preconceived notions about vampires. For most of us we didn't choose this any more than we chose to be human, but I really believe there's a place for all of us."

"So do I." The woman was all smiles.

Calla put her head on Isolde's shoulder, and the vampire let out a breath. "There's only the future, right?"

"Absolutely." Another woman laughed. "And it's so exciting, we get to witness history."

"We sure do." Calla smiled so wide her mouth hurt. "If you'll excuse me, I'm thirsty. Do you want a drink, baby?"

"Sure. I'll come with you." Isolde put her hand on Calla's back and they moved through the thinning crowd towards the small bar set up near the cash register. A selection of crime novels sat on the table. "What happened?" she whispered. Her usual stoic expression was gone, replaced with concern, and the change held Calla's attention, the way her eyebrows scrunched together, the downturn of her mouth.

"Fraction in the Council," Calla whispered, taking the cocktail the bartender offered.

"Just like the Directorate." She glanced around. "I know where you stand, but..."

"But this is a fucking mess and I should trust my captor?"

"Something like that. Cheers." Isolde held up her glass and Calla clinked hers against it. "Though your mother brought you into this, I dragged you deeper and I do feel a certain...responsibility for you. So, we'll talk later. With our words, not our fists, I hope."

"I make no promises. You know I like to hit."

"And I like to bite." Isolde smirked. "Okay, a few more rounds and then we'll leave."

Calla had refused help from Molly and instead stood in front of her mirror pulling pins from her hair. She looked at herself and found she looked the same as she ever did. While her world might be crumbling, she was still Calla Chase.

She settled into the chair in front of the vanity. Her mother had always been staunchly anti-vampire. When anyone brought up a desire to learn more about their ways, her mother would be the one to speak against it, rallying the hunters until going against her wasn't worth the effort. She always said they didn't need to know anything more than how to identify them. And Calla had agreed, it had been the one thing she and Gus had in common. They didn't want to know vampires, didn't want to learn anything except better ways to kill them.

But just a week in this strange place and she wasn't sure. Maybe they should have learned more. Or maybe she was being a fool. Isolde had killed people. Every vampire had killed someone. And not in the way Calla did, no matter what Isolde said. They killed innocents. Still, it was hard to be on the side of someone who was imprisoning her mother.

There was a knock on her door. "Come in." She didn't need to look to know it would be Isolde. She watched her enter through the mirror before turning. "We need to free my mom."

"Yes, I heard about that. I have been in contact with Aoife, she is one of the highest ranked members of the Directorate." Isolde walked across the room, no longer in her party dress, but a long cream-colored robe that brushed the floor.

Calla turned in her seat. "You knew?" Somehow the betrayal stung.

"Yes. I heard this morning. I intended to tell you tonight, I was hoping I could have her out before you learned of the situation. May I sit?"

Calla nodded. "You should have told me."

"I suppose. I assume what you wanted to tell me is what I just heard from Aoife. The Council is broken. There are those that support us—but not out of understanding, out of a desire to raise in their ranks in the world, and those that want to kill us. I do not know which group I fear more."

Calla thought of Naomi. She'd always hated how the Council was hidden, how all her good deeds went unnoticed. She didn't voice any of this to Isolde, instead she focused on the wall beyond her, out the window where the moonlight illuminated the estate grounds.

Isolde walked around the room, trailing her fingers over the furniture. "Thank you for tonight."

"What if I swear I will keep doing this, can I leave?"

Isolde stopped moving, and the two stared at each other for a long moment before she spoke. "Calla, it is not safe. Maybe this morning, maybe before we did this, but that horrid little man wants to make an example out of you."

"I can take care of myself."

"I know. I know that, but..." Isolde dragged her teeth along her bottom lip. "This is dangerous. It was always going to be dangerous for us to come out. Because of me it has gone more poorly than it should have. But it is even more dangerous for you. Not just Gus, not just the Council. You must understand that much of the world sees you as a liar. You knew of the supernatural, you knew of this great danger, and you lied to them."

Had she? She'd lied, but she'd always seen it as a way to keep people safe. She had been trained to do it from the cradle. Her lies protected people. She'd never considered how it kept them from protecting themselves. "I don't care. I want to leave."

"You can't. You made a deal."

"That did nothing because my mother—"

"Is currently being held by your own people! She is not on trial for murder. Her name is not in the press. I have held up my end of this agreement and I intend for you to do the same. You thought you would be nice for an evening and I would forget our agreement?"

Calla stood up, her body vibrating with frustration. "Sorry. You look like such a beautiful woman that sometimes I forget I'm talking to a piece of shit bloodsucker." She grabbed one of her makeup brushes and snapped it in her hand. "I'm not a plaything." She advanced on Isolde until her back was against the wall. Calla put the broken wood under her chin, lifting her head.

"I never thought you were" She held Calla's gaze in her own. "What's next, Calla?" Will you plunge that through my heart? Will you kill me for speaking the truth?"

"What do you want from me?" She pressed the wood to Isolde's throat until a trickle of blood appeared. "What do you want?" she screamed.

"Something I will never have." Isolde grabbed Calla's wrist, brushing her thumb down the veins along her arm. "Has anyone ever asked what you want, Calla? I could give it to you. I could give you so much."

Calla's fingers slipped, the stake clattered to the ground. There was nothing between them, just Isolde's fingers on her skin. "I know." She stepped back, but Isolde pulled her forward. She gripped Calla by the waist.

Heat filled her veins. The smell of Isolde was heavy in the air. "No." Calla moved away, too far for her to grab. "No." She turned and ran.

| Nine |

CALLA wasn't sure where she wanted to go. First, she started for the library, but she'd never be able to concentrate. What had just happened? She could still smell Isolde, feel the ghost of her fingers on her skin. And her question rang through her ears. What did Calla want? Had she ever known? She wanted to punch something. She could go to the training room, but the house reeked of Isolde.

She thought of the hourglass, the drops of blood, the unknowable magic of it. What was the truth? She had no idea. She could go back to the room where it had been, but she was sure it had been moved. So she slipped into a hallway she hadn't been in before and kept walking. There were gentle voices behind some of the doors. Why did these people work for Isolde? What was the thing she was not seeing?

The hallway ended with another door and she pushed it open to the cool night. The path was paved and lined with tall bushes. She kept walking, only just realizing she hadn't put on shoes. But it wasn't like she was going far. She wouldn't be able to walk home, and as much as she wanted to leave she knew walking alone in the middle of the night was not the solution.

Besides, what would wait for her at home? A battle for her mother. Fights with people she'd grown up training with? An absolute shitstorm was all the world had for Calla right now. Maybe it was a blessing she wasn't in the middle of it, that she hadn't been forced to pick a side. She knew she wouldn't want to fight under the leadership of Gus and she was no longer sure that being absolutely, unwaveringly anti-vampire was the right move for the world at large.

She had wanted to protect people; had foreseen none of this. People didn't need two overpowered groups fighting a war. They needed stability, not fear that vampires might jump out and bite them, that the Council might steal their loved ones if they disagreed, that Gus might do whatever came into his idiot brain with a slew of other muscled idiots behind him.

"Calla, what are you doing?" Isolde's voice made her jump.

Calla spun around, grinding her heel into the concrete. "Leave me alone."

"You're upset. You're running around in the middle of night."

"Well, that's rich from a vampire." Calla started to walk away but Isolde grabbed her arm. She hated how it made her feel to be touched by Isolde. She hated that Isolde could see it on her face. "Let me go."

"You can't go home, Calla. You can't go home because, in case you forgot, the Council paid for your apartment and they aren't doing that anymore. You don't have a home and..." She sighed and let go of Calla. But she was still too close. Brown eyes, pale skin, freckled even in the moonlight. "Please, can we be in this together? Let me help you."

"No." She couldn't. Never. It was too much.

"Shut up." Isolde pushed her. "You stupid, arrogant, child." She pushed her again, and Calla stumbled.

Then Calla laughed. She pushed Isolde back. "You kidnapping, life ruining, hoity-toity, asshole."

"You hot headed little shit." Isolde slammed her palms against Calla's shoulders. "You are so fucking annoying, do you know that? But oh, my staff just loves you. They won't shut up about it. They just love having a human here and—"

"Having a human?" Calla's intention to push Isolde back died. "You"—she pointed a finger at her—"don't know when to shut up. What does that mean?"

"What does *what* mean?" She took a step back. She was barefoot too, her toes tangled in the blades of grass. "They serve a vampire, you little idiot. They like working for a human."

"That's not what you meant." Calla resumed pushing her, making her take another step back and her feet sunk deeper into the dew-wet soil. "If your staff isn't human—"

"What? If they aren't human, then what? What, exactly, pray tell, do you intend to do?" Isolde stepped closer. There was a fleck of blood in the corner of her mouth. Her eyelashes were molten silver in the moonlight. "Will you call the Council? No, wait, there is no Council. Will you beat my staff into submission until they admit whatever falsehood you've made up in your mind? Tell me Calla, what on earth do you intend to do?"

Calla's arms dropped to her sides. "Fight."

The vampire never took her eyes off of Calla, holding her gaze as she moved ever closer, her voice low and smooth. "Why fight with me, Calla? The Council abandoned you, they set your mother up. We are outcasts from organizations we build up with our own hands. So work with me."

It was a tempting offer, a chance to start over. Part of Calla wished she was foolish enough to agree, if only to feel like she belonged again. "You know I can't. You are my captor. You are a liar. We could never be on the same team."

Isolde stepped back, into the shadows of the house looming behind her. "Do you know how hard it is to be seen as a monster? To spend your life in the dark? I have not felt the sun on my skin in centuries."

"That is only a sob story. It changes nothing." Calla wrapped her arms around herself as the wind blew through the yard. "Tell me one truth."

"Will it matter?" Isolde asked.

"It might." Calla glanced up at the moon. What would it be like to live only under its light?

"Then come, we will go inside. You are cold." But Isolde did not walk back towards the door Calla had fled through. She followed the bushes outside the estate. "I will show you a secret."

And Calla knew she was trying, but she did not think it would ever be enough. Though Isolde might be a victim in her own way, she was still a vampire. She would always be a vampire and Calla would always be a hunter. She could feel Isolde in her soul, the way being around her made her heart beat faster, her hairs stand on end. Calla could feel the danger she posed, and no matter how wide her brown eyes got, no matter how sad her story, Calla had been bred to destroy her.

Yet she followed the footsteps she left on the dewy grass until Isolde stopped, seemingly at random, in front of one of the many gargoyles on the property. "A secret before a truth," she said and pressed one of its wings down.

What Calla had taken for a solid stone wall swung forward and Isolde stepped inside. Calla hesitated. Not following a vampire into a strange, dark passage seemed like Hunter 101, but curiosity won and the door swung shut behind her.

For a moment they were plunged into darkness, and then electric sconces ignited, illuminating a long hallway. Embarrassingly, Calla let out a little squeak.

Isolde laughed. "Some hunter. They're motion activated."

The hallway was longer than Calla would have guessed, and she felt like she was inside the bowels of the house. She could hear things moving on the other side of the wall, electronics buzzing, but she had no idea where they were. Isolde knew the path well, opening up more secret passages in the stone wall with a brush of her finger until Calla was absolutely certain she'd made a mistake.

All the vulnerable moments had been a trick to lead her here, where Isolde was most certainly going to eat her. The vampire pushed open a door in the wall and light flooded the tunnel. Yep, Calla was about to be a midnight snack.

The kitchen was enormous and immaculate. The stainless steel appliances contrasted with the rest of the room, which still had the original brick and wood, all in perfect condition. Isolde walked across the floor, leaving dirty footprints, grabbed a wine glass, and pulled the fridge open, disappearing behind its massive door.

"I think my entire kitchen would fit in your fridge."

"Your fridge now." Isolde stood straight, her glass full of burgundy liquid.

"Me too." Calla nodded towards the glass.

"The wine is in the cooler under the island. You don't want this. Or maybe you do." She swirled the glass and Calla could feel herself blush at the mistake. She busied herself with getting wine.

She grabbed a bottle older than she was and took a deep breath before standing. Trying to stay angry with Isolde all the time was exhausting. She rooted around in the drawers until she found a corkscrew, pulled out the cork, and brought the bottle to her lips.

"No." Isolde grabbed her arm. "That is not some swill from the grocery store. You do not drink it from the bottle. A glass, you heathen." She grabbed one from overhead and took the bottle from Calla. "If you want to drink from a bottle, I know Beatrix has tequila stashed around here somewhere."

"I'll stick to this." She plucked the glass from Isolde's fingers. She was always so close, always inside Calla's personal space. "You promised me a truth."

Isolde put her glass of blood on the counter and pushed herself up to sit beside it. Her robe fell open to her thighs, exposing more of her than Calla had seen. "As I said, and as I'm sure you suspected, they set your mother up. Some of the Council, the part now led by Naomi, and some of the Directorate knew."

"You let her kill your friend?" Calla leaned against the counter.

"No. I was against the plan from the start, and it was not that simple. We only knew she was angry, acting irrationally. They got the idea from what happened to me. We had her followed. It was only a matter of time."

"To blackmail me?"

"To blackmail all of you. To have something to show if you speak against us."

Calla digested the information, downing her glass of wine in the process. "Why would the Council do that?"

98

"To get rid of some of its most volatile members." Isolde leaned across Calla and poured her another glass. The smell of smoke filled Calla's nose. She imagined her, robe-clad, smoking a cigar. Vampires probably didn't worry about cancer too much.

"What about you? Did the Directorate know?"

"I suspect they did. I can't prove anything. I am also a... volatile member. I think they hoped the two of us would kill each other. Another truth—I do not think they ever wanted me. I think they only wanted what I provided, a descendant of the original line."

"How can that be? Wouldn't you have all come from the same lineage?"

Isolde shrugged and drained her glass. She refilled it with wine. "I don't know. Maybe my maker did, but I never really got to know him, just Braccio, another he made, and much later. The king had my sire killed at some point after he made me, or so I've heard."

The alcohol was going to Calla's head. She hadn't eaten much lately. "How many humans have you killed?"

Isolde clicked her tongue. "I think that's enough truths from me. How about some from you?"

Calla nodded, but moved back, sliding down in front of the fridge until she was sitting. "But first, do I really not have a house?"

"No." Isolde jumped from the counter with inhuman grace and agility and sat on the floor across from Calla. The soles of her feet were filthy. "That part was not my doing. That was all the dissident Council."

Homeless. Calla had never had a job. The Council had always paid her bills and given her living money. What the fuck was she going to do now? Live with a vampire apparently, because she doubted the Council would let her live with Lisbet, and she didn't have many other friends. "Go ahead. Ask me a question."

"Do you sleep with women?"

Calla coughed into her glass and had to wipe the wine off her chin. Whatever she had been expecting, that wasn't it. "Yeah, I do. Not that it's mattered since you guys came out." When the vampires had lived in the shadows, Calla had never had a problem keeping her bed warm. Now people found out what she did and wanted no part of it. She had tried to hide that part of herself, but somehow they always figured it out.

"Well, I apologize that me joining society has made it harder for you to get laid. Welcome to the world of being a vampire."

"Oh, please. You look like Malibu Barbie meets Elsa Schiaparelli. You're hot and spooky." Jesus, she'd had too much to drink. She reached above her head to grab the bottle and poured more. "This is good."

"Indeed. And you are incorrect—not about me being hot and spooky." Isolde smirked. "But not being able to go out in the daylight, not being able to eat food, having these teeth. It makes it hard. Obviously I can get laid, but sometimes I want more."

"Stop trying to bond with me." Calla tried to look cross.

"You're an asshole, you know that? I tell you how hard it is to connect with people and you tell me not to try to bond with you. Maybe I should put you out, let you wander the streets homeless and see how you like it. I can assure you, it is awful. Do you think I wanted some angry, human girl in my house?"

"Oh, you enjoy having me in your house. I can see it in your face. You like arguing with me." Calla scooted closer. Isolde was right. She was homeless. Plus, she hadn't gotten laid in months. Half the Council wanted her dead. Her mother was locked up. She was drunk. She was trapped in a vampire's house. She felt like she was standing on the edge of a cliff and wanted to jump, if only to feel like she was flying. "

"What are you doing?" Isolde tried to back away but there was solid wood behind her.

"Don't you? You like having me in your house?" She would blow the whole thing up. She was so tired of following the rules.

"Yes," Isolde said, her eyes on Calla's neck.

She swept her hair back. "Do you want to bite me? How does it taste?"

"Calla, stop."

She moved closer, their knees touched. "Do you think it would sell it? If I showed up with the mark of your mouth on my neck?" She leaned closer. Smoke and blood and wine.

Isolde stood up. "You're drunk."

And she left.

Calla flopped back against the floor. Why had she done that? She would have liked to pretend she didn't know, but she did. She needed Isolde to be the bad guy. She needed her to give in to a moment of temptation. To prove vampires were exactly what she thought they were. To give Calla relief against all the things she'd been feeling since she stepped foot into the house.

But she hadn't. She'd left. And Calla had, once again, been the jerk.

| Ten |

THE bottle of wine was empty. Calla pushed herself up and grabbed another. She wasn't normally one to drown her sorrows but nothing about her life was normal.

She'd stuck her neck out in front of a vampire, and the vampire had walked away. So much for uncontrollable blood lust. She could add that to the list of bullshit she'd been raised on.

The house was quiet, but not silent. She could still hear the scurry of staff. Did they keep vampire hours as well? She took another drink and creeped into the hallway. The last thing she wanted was to see anyone, so she hid in the shadows from every noise until she was in the library.

The lights were off and the room was silent. She stood at the entrance, making sure it stayed that way and then she walked in. Somewhere nearby was the hourglass. The magic brushed against her. She wanted to scream, to knock over every shelf and burn the library to the ground. She wanted to cry.

The world was closing in. Gus wanted to kill her. Calla had wanted to slap the shit out of him more times than she could count. But to actually hurt him? Not once, not a single time, had Calla thought of actually hurting another hunter. But a group of them wanted her dead for something she'd barely had a choice about.

Except she had. She could have said no. She could have let her mother go to trial. She could have dealt with the consequences. They had threatened her with even more loss when she was vulnerable and she'd fallen right into the trap.

God, she was a complete fucking disaster right now. Maybe she should find Gus and rough him up a little. This was the longest she'd gone since she was a child without a proper fight and it was setting her on edge. She needed violence, something tangible to direct her anger at.

She looked at the books. She didn't want them seeing her like this, so she left the library and headed towards the stairs, fully intending to find Isolde, but instead found herself lost.

"Fuck." Calla opened a door and a stack of linens tumbled out. "Isolde!" she yelled, and it echoed down the hallway. "I apologize!" She shoved the linens back in the closet and kept walking. The next hallway was more familiar, but she wasn't sure how it connected to the wing of the house Isolde slept in. "Isolde!"

"Stop yelling and hold on." Her voice came from somewhere below Calla.

She stopped walking, the bottle of wine dangling from her fingers. "You better hurry because I'm drinking straight from the bottle."

"What?" Isolde came around a corner, but was still far away because her house was too fucking big. "Listen, I don't know what that was—"

"Fight me." Calla took another drink.

"What?" Isolde tried to take the bottle. Calla moved out of her reach. "You're drunk. Give me that."

"I need to fight. I fight. It's what I do. It's who I am. That's why I've been feeling this way." She wasn't made for book readings and balls and servants. She was made for brawls.

"You feel this way because you drank a bottle and a half of wine in like half an hour." She reached out again, and again Calla danced out of her reach.

"Come on, Izzy. You know you enjoyed wrestling with me. Gets your blood pumping. Come on." She put the bottle on a table. "Fight me." Calla brought her fists up.

"First of all, I don't box." Isolde was still in her robe, but the tie was loosening, revealing more skin each time she moved.

"Catch me, then." Calla feigned right and tried to take off down the hallway. She got about three steps before Isolde was on her back, her legs wrapped around Calla's waist.

"Not hard." Her lips were at the shell of Calla's ear. "And now what? Your whole neck is exposed. Some hunter you—"

Calla flipped Isolde off of her, and she landed on the ground with a thud, her blonde hair sprawled across the rug. Calla moved to get on top of her, but Isolde had vampire speed and she was up before Calla hit the floor, sending her off balance. Calla's knees hit the ground hard, but she stopped herself with her hands, scrambling away just as Isolde had, but the vampire grabbed her by the ankle.

Calla kicked out, making contact with Isolde's chest and she let out a grunt but didn't let go. She was stronger, older than most of the vampires Calla fought, and she dragged her across the carpet.

Calla grabbed the leg of a table and twisted herself free. "Bloodsucker." She swung, connecting with the side of Isolde's head. The vampire returned the blow, leaving Calla's vision blurry. She brought a hand to her jaw. "Ouch."

"Are you done?" Isolde's breathing was heavy. Without warning, she leapt at Calla, knocking her to the ground. And yet again the hunter found herself beneath the vampire.

"You asked if I was done! That's cheating!" Calla contemplated all the ways she could knock Isolde off of her, but getting punched in the face had sobered her up a bit.

"Calla whatever-your-middle-name-is Chase, I was planning to tell you that there's a gala for the Vampire Human Alliance tomorrow and I'd like you to go. Now you're going to have a bruise. I don't want you to have a bruise. It won't look nice."

"Oh, you wanted to ask me?" Calla pushed herself up onto her elbows. "Am I free to make my own choices now? Maybe I can even dress myself."

"Well, you just punched me in the face for no reason, which was a choice." Isolde lowered herself until their noses were almost touching, her thighs on either side of Calla.

"So, we meet again." Calla grinned and maybe she wasn't entirely sober yet. "You, me, a wrestling match. The ground. Some things never change." She kissed Isolde's forehead. "Thank you for indulging me. No, I would not like to go to the gala with you, but have a spectacular time!" She tried to wiggle free, but Isolde held firm.

"No. You have to come."

"There it is." She moved suddenly, throwing Isolde off balance enough that she was able to get out from under her, but she stayed on the ground, staring up at the ceiling.

Isolde sighed and laid down beside her, their shoulders touching. "Fine, you don't have to go. Stay here. I'll go to the Vampire Human Alliance, learn all kinds of intel, and you'll be here, at my house, by yourself, not dancing with me."

"What the fuck is the Vampire Human Alliance?"

"Some bullshit made up by the Directorate, but there will be a bunch of human leaders and rich assholes. They aren't even pretending it's charity, it's just a way for everyone to rub elbows and get to know each other. You *should* be there. Meet some world leaders. Network."

"I've always wanted to catfish a billionaire."

"That's the spirit." Isolde sighed. "Calla?"

"Hmm?"

"Please come. You are, unfortunately, the closest thing I have to a friend or an ally right now. I..." Isolde didn't finish her sentence, she propped herself up on one elbow, looking at Calla.

Somewhere nearby someone started vacuuming. It almost made Calla laugh, being in the estate felt like going back in time. She turned onto her side and looked at Isolde. She wanted to be angry, to feel the hatred she usually felt when she looked at her, but she didn't. Despite the fact that Isolde was obviously lying about so much, despite the fact that the two of them would never be able to truly trust each other. Despite it all, what Isolde had said was true. Calla had one friend, Lisbet, and with everything going on she didn't know if she could really trust her.

She had her mom as an ally, she never doubted that, but she was locked up and Calla had no way of getting to her. So she had Isolde. She was sure Isolde would protect her, for whatever reason she needed Calla around. It wasn't friendship, and it wasn't trust, but it was more than she had from most people right now.

She didn't press Isolde for the rest of her sentence. She didn't need to know all her secrets. "How does this end, Isolde? Do you really think I can get the whole world to trust you?"

"No." She frowned, her gaze dropping from Calla to the floor. "Not at all."

"You could tell me the truth. I know you haven't."

"Unfortunately, I cannot."

Calla nearly reached out to her, nearly put her hand on Isolde's shoulder. But she didn't. "Fine."

"No, Calla. I *cannot*."

"Oh." The truth settled like a stone in Calla. Magic. Old magic. She knew little about magic, but she knew it lingered. Curses that were never undone. Blessings that still graced the families they were bestowed upon. Witch artifacts. "Do the others know?"

Isolde glanced up and then back at the floor.

Well, that was a delicious little tidbit. It felt like an olive branch. Something Calla had that even the other vampires did not. And *fuck*. She squeezed her eyes shut and breathed deep. She had been sure she would hate Isolde, that she would have an outlet for her rage and hatred. It should have been easy, Isolde had been so glib and stuck-up. But the more time Calla spent with her the more lonely Isolde seemed.

When she opened her eyes, she stared at the ceiling, not trusting herself to look at Isolde. How was there no dust up there? The ceiling fan in her apartment was filthy, but there wasn't even the beginnings of a cobweb in the entire house.

All of this could be an act. Part of Calla hoped it was. She wanted to be right, to go back to her old feelings. Vampires were bad, and she was the good that fought them. That was simple. Right now, lying on the floor side by side with Isolde, nothing seemed simple at all. It all seemed so fucking complicated.

"I'll go," Calla said. What other option was there? The world was moving forward. There was no going back to the before. Whether or not Isolde was lying, she would need a life after this, a job. She might as well meet some people who might help her with that.

When Calla finally glanced over, Isolde was still looking at her, a curious expression Calla couldn't figure out on her face. She knew she should look away, but she couldn't. Instead she looked back, into brown eyes that had seen centuries. Her skin was smooth, perfect and unblemished. Isolde could not have been much older than twenty when she was turned. "What was it like, back when you were human."

"Awful," Isolde said. "Maybe not for everyone but for me. My family had been wealthy generations back, but most of it was dried up by the time I came around. They were selling daughters off as assets. I thought being the king's mistress would save me from marrying some old, awful man. I traded one villain for another and it got me killed. I can't even blame his wife. Queens could be killed for the sin of no longer being new. She had children to protect."

"I was eleven the first time I fought a vampire," Calla said. "I nearly died, but he was newly turned. Sometimes we do die, no one ever talks about it but hunter children die. They have no use for us if we aren't good fighters. And yet, not all of them have to do it. Gus is only a descendant of hunters. He has none of our powers. He's a good fighter for a human, and he's killed a few vampires, but no one made him fight at eleven. They listen to him. He's got real power and I have..."

"I'm sure they call it glory."

"They do. But it's murder, and it's heavy when you're a child." Calla had not talked about her first kill in years. She'd barely spoken of it then and never admitted the rest. She wasn't sure why she was even saying it now, there was no peace Isolde could offer.

Isolde was still staring at her. "When I was first changed, I didn't understand anything. I ran as soon as I could, before I knew anything, and I just... I killed too many people. I couldn't control it. Once I could, once the blood lust cooled, those deaths were heavy too. I know it's not the same but... I don't know, I understand, at least a little."

Calla nodded. "Maybe it will be better one day. For all the little girls who won't have to fight."

"I hope so."

When Calla woke she was glad she was alone. Someone, probably Molly, had left breakfast on her desk but her head and stomach both hurt, reminding her of all the wine she had drank last night. She tried not to remember the way she had stared into a vampire's eyes, how she had shared secrets she'd never revealed before.

She clicked her phone on, not expecting anything, but she had a text from Lisbet.

Can you get out of your deal?

Then another minutes later.

Ignore me. Just spitballing. Working on getting your mom out. Had a meeting with Gus. I'm not pro-vampire but he's really lost it.

Calla tapped her fingers on her phone. What was there to even say? She wasn't sure she wanted to leave. She didn't know where she would live. But she had to say something.

Let me know if there's anything I can do to help. I miss you. Happy to see a text.

She pulled a brush through her hair and then eyed the food on the plate. She managed to eat two pieces of bacon before she felt too nauseous to continue. Her phone lit up.

I've been staying with a friend. Hard to believe I can't trust the Council anymore. Shit, they probably have my phone bugged.

Calla wanted to laugh, but she worried it was true. She texted back a non-committal answer then powered her phone down. She wanted to stay in touch, but what if they were reading what she said? The human government was pretty liberal with letting the Council decide punishment for members. Would she be the next to be locked up?

Someone knocked on her door. "I appreciate—" It wasn't Molly in the open doorway but Isolde. "Hey."

"You look terrible." Isolde laughed and stepped through the threshold.

"Thanks." Calla glanced towards the window. She had been up most of the night and now it was already early afternoon. "Doesn't it bother you?"

Isolde shook her head. "No, it can't scorch me through glass, but it does get very toasty if I get too close." She walked to Calla's wardrobe and opened it, running her hands on all the dresses.

"Hands off the clothes, bloodsucker," Calla said, but there was no bite to her voice. "Seriously, what are you doing?"

"Well, if you're going to be my date you need to look nice. You can wear the black one. You looked beautiful in it." She touched the first dress Calla had tried on at the shop. "I'll wear red. We'll look great."

Calla crossed the room and pushed the wardrobe shut. "Would you let me leave? If I packed my things and tried to go—"

Isolde caught Calla in her gaze, her brown eyes wide and deep like tilled earth. "I would stop you. I would bring you back." She took a strand of Calla's hair between her fingers. "I would keep you."

"Why?" Calla's heart beat an unsteady rhythm. "Why me? You could have picked any human."

"Because I want *you,* and I always get what I want."

The air was thick. Calla struggled to pull it into her lungs. "I don't think you can have me."

"Then no one else will have you, Calla. I could not bear it." Isolde dropped the strand of Calla's hair and put her hand on her waist, pulling her close. "But I think I can have you. I think you want me too, even though you wish you didn't."

Calla watched her lips move, the hint of sharp teeth beneath them. "I'm a hunter. I could not love a vampire."

Something flashed in Isolde's eyes, and then she recovered. She brushed her nose against Calla's neck and whispered in her ear, "Who speaks of love? I talk only of desire. Do you not desire me, Calla?"

There was a choice to make, an opportunity to give in, to forget everything for at least a moment. Instead, Calla pulled back and Isolde's hand dropped from her waist. "I can't, Isolde. You're..."

Isolde smiled, but it did not reach her eyes. "I am a vampire and you are a hunter. I know."

Just another step back. Just a little more space between them. But Calla could not get her feet to move. "But... we can pretend. Tonight. We can pretend it could be real for us too." She thought the words would help her catch her breath, but they only tightened the vice around her heart.

"The black dress, then," Isolde said, and she was gone, pulling the door behind her.

Calla pressed her forehead to the wardrobe. There were moments when Isolde seemed human, vulnerable and kind. But she was a vampire. She was dangerous and territorial. And she was right. Calla had been ignoring it since the moment she had seen her, but she wanted Isolde. She didn't want to. She'd pluck Isolde from her brain if she could, but she could not pretend the vampire didn't stir feelings in her. That she did not wonder what she would taste like, how she might feel beneath Isolde's no doubt skilled hands.

She pushed herself up, the bacon doing somersaults in her stomach, and opened the wardrobe. The dress was beautiful and whatever she felt she was going to the gala tonight. She was going to keep living in the estate. And every day it felt like she had less and less to lose.

| Eleven |

"HOLD still," Molly whacked her shoulder with the hairbrush. "You're moving around like you have ants in your pants."

She wasn't far off from the truth. Calla felt like she was going to crawl out of her skin. She needed fresh air. She needed to scream. She needed to go back in time a few hours and not promise a fucking vampire she could take her on a date.

It really had been too long since she'd gotten laid.

Calla looked into the mirror. "You're a miracle worker." She looked a million times better than she felt. Molly had curled her hair and threaded crystals through it, a universe of twinkling stars. Her makeup was perfect. Her palms were clammy.

"I have a beautiful canvas." Molly sat on the vanity and looked down at Calla. "Though I try not to meddle, I couldn't help but overhearing some of the conversations between you and Mistress Isolde." She took Calla's hand in her own. "You are a good girl. I do not know your mother, but I can see how well you were raised. And as I've told you before, there is no shame in change. Do not look at yourself in the mirror as though you are a monster. You are a masterpiece."

"Why are you so nice to me?"

"Because your mother is not here and you often look like you could use a mother. And because I have seen Isolde suffer and stress trying to bring change only to have it fall down around her. I care about her and I am learning to care about you." She squeezed Calla's hand. "Would you not wish me happiness?"

"I would, even though you helped kidnap me."

"Psh." Molly dropped her hand and stood back up. "I had no part in that. I am a simple housekeeper. And I believe you helped kidnap yourself, love. Okay, you're ready."

"I don't think I am. I think I've made a huge mistake."

"No. No. None of that." Molly placed her hands firmly on Calla's shoulders. "You are doing the best you can with the horrible situation you've found yourself in. But tonight, you are going to dance, drink a little less than last night and have fun. Okay?"

"Okay." Calla nodded and her curls bobbed. "I deserve to be at the Vampire Human Alliance."

"Damn right you do. Now get out of here!" Molly gave her a little shove, and with a deep breath and shaking nerves, Calla headed out of her room and towards the door. At the top of the stairs she stopped, squeezing the stair railing so hard she worried it might crack.

Isolde was at the bottom of the stairs, dressed in red as she had promised. She didn't have on her usual hat, instead her hair was set in curls like Calla's. The dress was timeless, with a wide skirt and a tight bodice. Long, ruby earrings dangled from Isolde's ears brushing the sides of her neck.

As Calla made her way down the stairs, all the things Isolde had said to her came back, making her toes curl in her shoes. Did she want Calla as badly as Calla wanted her? Did she wish she didn't? Was she lonely? Was that why she sometimes seemed like a different person? Why she spilled herself to Calla?

114

Calla felt lightheaded when she paused at the bottom step, and Isolde closed the distance between them. "Just for tonight?" She offered Calla her arm.

"Just for tonight," Calla said, taking it and following her to the car.

The drive to the gala was short. The venue was outside the city in an enormous old house that had been converted to an events center a decade ago. When she ignored all the bad parts, Calla felt like she was in a dream. A beautiful woman, a fancy party, an expensive dress. All the parts of life that Calla saw in movies but never got because her life was in the shadows, because she never wanted to draw attention to herself.

Beatrix got out before they did and pulled the door open. She smirked when Calla got out. "Have fun."

"I will." Calla turned to help Isolde out of the car as others streamed inside. She'd already recognized several politicians.

A banner above the entrance read HUMAN VAMPIRE ALLIANCE INAUGURAL GALA. Calla smiled up at it. This was the most outrageous thing she'd ever done. A year ago she never would have imagined herself here, but she couldn't fight it any longer. Might as well lean into the weirdness that her life had become.

If the Council didn't want her, then she'd figure this out. She had skills; she was smart and resourceful. She could be an assent in so many ways.

"Are you ready?" she whispered to Isolde as they ascended the stairs.

"You look beautiful," Isolde responded, and they walked through the door together.

Inside, the gala was stunning, almost tastefully done in cream and jewel tones except that Calla could tell it had cost someone a fortune. The lights were low, and for a moment Calla's stomach clenched, the scent of vampires thick in the air. But she glanced at Isolde and allowed herself to relax. Tonight was not for fighting.

"Oh, Isolde!" Someone called, and they both turned, arm in arm to find a woman Calla had only ever seen in social media pictures. Andie Yost had once been the face of social media, creating one of the most downloaded apps ever. Then she'd sold it for billions. Now Calla wasn't sure what she did except for being obscenely rich.

"Andie. It's fantastic to see you. This is Calla Chase, former vampire hunter. Current vampire's girlfriend."

Instead of clenching, Calla's stomach swooped. "It's a pleasure to meet you." She shook Andie's hand. She even smelled expensive.

"And you. Vampire hunting. That must have been fascinating. Listen, I've got a few people I need to say hi to, but I'd love to talk more later. There's a story there!" She smiled wide and then was gone, swept away in the crowd.

"Drinks or dancing?" Isolde asked.

"Dancing. I already feel drunk," Calla said. She wanted to be tough, to pretend none of this meant anything to her but her heart was racing and her mind was floating. And maybe, just maybe, tonight could just be a nice memory to have in the sea of bullshit she'd been going through. For tonight, maybe she could stop fighting and just live.

"Good." Isolde's hand slipped from her arm to her hand and she pulled her through the crowd, into a larger room. *A ballroom.* Calla had never been in a ballroom in her life, and Isolde had danced in the halls of kings.

A band played, but Calla could barely see them through the crowd of people. Actors and Prime Ministers rubbed elbows with vampires on every side of her. She dragged her eyes away from them as her hands found their way to Isolde's hips, swaying to the music. "I don't know any dances. Like waltzes or anything."

Isolde smiled. "I could teach you, but I think this is fine for now." Her arms were around Calla's shoulders, hooked behind her neck.

Looking into Isolde's face, her brown eyes lined with thick lashes, her full lips, Calla knew she should be mad. Isolde had trapped her. But she had also saved her, had seen what was coming and pulled Calla out of it before she could get tangled up in the wreckage of her life. And the way Isolde was looking at her—like no one else was in the room—made her heart, and other things, ache.

There was something so delicious about an ancient vampire, a really hot seven hundred-year-old vampire, having a crush on her. Wanting her. She had fought vampires all her life, this was taboo, it was wrong. It was, undeniably, hot.

"What are you thinking? You have a look," Isolde asked, her voice low.

Calla let her hands drop, brushing the top of Isolde's ass. She'd given herself tonight, after all. She might as well use the free pass. "What if we found an empty room? What would it be like? Would you *bite*?" She tugged Isolde closer, pressing their bodies together.

Isolde's tongue darted out, wetting her bottom lip before disappearing. "Only if you wanted me to. I've had many lovers, Calla. I've learned *many* things."

"How long do we need to be here?" Calla pressed her thighs together. Maybe she did need a drink.

"We—"

"Isolde, I didn't expect to see you here." Another vampire stood beside them. Calla had forgotten where she was, that she was supposed to be networking. Briefly, she considered all the ways she could stake the interloper.

"Biyu." Isolde pulled away from Calla. "You know I love to surprise."

The dark-haired vampire laughed. "Hugo will be most disappointed. Sometimes I think he hopes you fail. And you know I love to see him disappointed. This must be the human."

"Some people even call me Calla."

"A hunter though, 'Solde? Do you not worry?" Biyu looked Calla up and down. "Certainly it would be easier with a more malleable counterpart."

"I have never desired malleability," Isolde said.

"And do you think you will complete everything you hoped to accomplish?"

Calla had been on the verge of reminding Biyu that she was standing there but now she stopped moving, trying to breathe as quietly as she could, to fade away and hope the vampires forgot she was present. Had Isolde been telling her the truth? Was it really her job to enamour the public with vampires? And if so, what was the thing she could not tell her? The mystery deepened.

"I think a great percentage of the humans already love us. How are things going on your end?" Isolde asked, her eyes stayed on Biyu but her fingers brushed Calla's shoulder blades.

"I am working on it tonight. I'm going to attempt some international appearances. Your book was a hit. I told Aoife we had nothing to worry about but—" Her eyes cut to Calla and she felt like she was in a spotlight.

"I..." Was she supposed to tell her?

"Oh, I'm sure she's told you every vampire secret so I don't know why I hesitate. We told her not to, but she's tender-hearted. As old as she is, I swear Isolde has twice the feelings of other vampires. More human now than before she was turned."

"Stop." But miraculously Isolde was blushing.

"Well, I'll let you get back to canoodling. You better hope there's a photographer around because the way the two of you were looking at each other would certainly convince a few people hunters had changed their tune. Or at least one had." Biyu winked, threw her hair over her shoulder and left.

"Well, that's Biyu," Isolde said. "Her five hundredth birthday is coming up. She's working on getting it televised internationally."

"I assume I'll be going to that," Calla said, trying to sound annoyed but there was a little tingle of excitement down her spine. Five hundred years. How deep the relationships of vampires must be.

"If you can manage another night with me. Congressman Zimmer!" Isolde waved her hand above her head. "He's a creep but his constituents love him," she hissed.

"I'm going to get drinks. I'm not great with sleaz—Hello Congressman Zimmer! I was just about to go grab a glass of champagne, would you like one?" Calla asked.

The slick-haired man looked her over, hitching his thumbs in his belt loops. "You don't look like a waitress."

"Indeed, I am not. And you don't—"

"We'd love the drinks, darling! Tell me, Henry, how is your wife? I've heard she's been spending the season in Belize."

"Well, you know how marriage can be."

Calla didn't need to hear anymore. She wove through the crowd towards the bar at the back. "Do you have beer?"she asked, leaning across the polished wood. "And maybe a shot of something strong?"

"Not having a good time?" The bartender stopped in front of her.

"Having a weird time."

He poured a shot of whiskey, which was not Calla's favorite, but she downed it. "And beer?"

"Sorry, no beer. Did I see you dancing with Isolde? You're the girl I've been hearing about. A hunter. How did that happen?"

"Ummm. I'll take two glasses of champagne, and I don't know. I mean... have you seen her?" She glanced through the crowd, but she couldn't make out Isolde from where she was. "Plus, she's funny and... well, it's kind of exhilarating. Sometimes she's terrifying and sometimes she's sweet, and who doesn't like a little excitement?"

"Well, good for you. I think that would be too much excitement for me. Maybe some of the others but she's a big one. Everyone knows her name." He placed two glasses in front of her.

And the room exploded.

| Twelve |

CALLA grabbed the bar, her ears ringing. Took a deep breath. She was a hunter. She was Calla Chase. She kicked off her shoes and ran through the crowd. People were screaming. She struggled to stay upright.

What the fuck was going on?

Another scream. This one the scream of someone in pain. Someone dying. She pushed through people heading towards the exit, nearly crashing into Andie Yost, who was bleeding from her nose. She needed to find Isolde. What had been the door of the ballroom was now a gaping wound of wood. Someone had set off a bomb. Fuck.

She knew how to fight vampires, but she wasn't much use against explosives. She stopped and someone running by knocked into her shoulder hard enough to hurt. "What's going on?" she yelled but they kept moving.

And then she got her answer, because she recognized some of the faces moving through the crowd, stakes and guns in hand. "Hey!" Calla screamed, preparing herself to fight hunters. "There are people here! Humans! We don't hurt humans."

"Calla." Gus stepped out in front of her. Of course. She should have anticipated the fish in a barrel allure of the event, but she had been too wrapped up in the thrill.

"Why?" Calla hated the tremble in her voice, but the room was still smoking and people were screaming, bleeding, dying all around her.

"*Why?* You really have forgotten our mission." Gus moved his hand but Calla was quicker, she had always been quicker. She kicked the knife away before he could fully grasp it. It went flying, clattering against the cracked marble floor where couples had been dancing only minutes before.

She swung. He dodged but stumbled, knocking into a table behind him. Calla had him, though she wasn't sure what she was going to do with him. She stepped closer, blocking his exit. "This isn't the way. Destruction? Mass casualties. You can't think this is what we were trained to do."

"Fucking vampires isn't what we were trained to do," Gus said, venom in his voice. "I saw you dancing. I saw the way you looked at her. The way she touched you. Once I thought we could lead the Council—you and I. But not now. You're unclean."

This time when Calla swung her fist collided with his mouth, and his lip split, blood splattering. "You are a fool." She glanced around, looking for a way to restrain him. Isolde's voice cut through the chaos, calling her name.

She forgot about Gus as she spun around, running into the smoke. "Isolde!" She could barely see, something was still on fire and the closer she got to the site of the explosion the hotter the temperature rose. The smoke stung her eyes and clawed at her lungs.

She tripped over something and fell onto the corpse of the congressman Isolde had been talking to. She had to be nearby. "Isolde!" She scrambled to her feet, trying to think of anything but the dead body, not wanting it burned into her memory.

Isolde called her name again, her voice muffled and still far away. Calla looked around but the smoke was too thick to see more than a foot in front of her face, so she walked blindly in the direction of her voice.

Flames licked at the doorway. Calla braced herself, hoped for the best, and ran until she was through the heat and into a hallway where the chaos only continued. People were screaming for their loved ones. People were fighting. She recognized more hunters. Each face broke her heart. This was a bastardization of their mission, of everything they had believed in. Everything she had believed in.

She spun around until she saw a blur of red dress and blonde hair and she ran again. A hunter had her arms around Isolde's waist dragging her. She clawed at her trying to get away, but she was bleeding heavily from her head, her leg was bruised and, Calla suspected, broken.

"Elise!" She yelled at the hunter, her heart racing. Gus was nothing, a powerless son of a hunter. But Elise was a true hunter with power rivaling Calla's.

Elise stopped and Isolde's eyes found Calla's, recognition blooming without hope, before her head fell to the side. "Oh no. Looks like your girlfriend has lost too much blood. What a funny way for a vampire to go."

"Are you serious?" Calla moved slowly, trying to come up with a plan. "The Council made me do this. I was saving my mother."

"Naomi is no true member of the Council. And she was no ally to you. Your mother wanted to free you and Naomi could not let that happen. She has always been a vamp sympathizer, we all knew it. You should have refused. We would have found a way to help you both. But there is still time. Help me bring in the rest of these vamps. There is division in their ranks as well, they will be an easy target."

They were close to the exit. If Elise got Isolde outside, Calla was sure more hunters were waiting. Gus was still around somewhere. She needed to do something now. She needed to get out of the smoky building.

The faint sound of sirens hit her ears. Fire trucks or police. Calla couldn't tell. And whose side would they be on? What side was *she* on?

In Elise's arms, Isolde made a small whimpering noise. Blood flowed down her face, matting her hair. But her body was limp, her eyes closed. Could vampires die of blood loss? She'd certainly be easy for the Council to kill right now, or worse, drag into the Council headquarters and torture.

And Calla knew whose side she was on. "Elise, let her go. You don't want to fight me." Elise's skills might rival Calla's but they weren't better. "You blew up a ballroom. You just did wonders for the vampire's public image, you fucking degenerate." She moved even closer, trying to get within striking distance. "Is Gus your leader? You're taking orders from Gus fucking Cadieux and wonder why I didn't join you?"

Uncertainty played across Elise's face. "We had to do something."

"Did it have to be this mind numbingly stupid?" Calla asked. Elise was off balance with Isolde's dead weight in her arms. If she could get one of her feet out from under her she could grab Isolde and then—

And then what? Was she going to knock Elise unconscious? Kill a hunter? Elise glanced over her shoulder and Calla lunged forward, grabbing Isolde with one arm and catching's Elise's foot with her own. The hunter went down and Isolde's weight fell onto Calla, knocking her over as well.

"Fuck." She tried to push herself up, but Elise was above her. Without Isolde hindering her she was faster than Calla.

A face appeared over her shoulder and Calla could have wept with relief as Lisbet wrapped her arms around Elise's neck and held tight. "Nighty night, you little shit." When Elise's eyes closed, Lisbet let her body drop to the floor. "That's for kissing David Ziegler in middle school."

She offered Calla a hand but Calla shook her head, looking at Isolde. She couldn't die. Calla had just found her. The sirens were louder.

"Calla, we have to go. I don't know what's going to happen, but I don't think we should be here."

"She's right." Beatrix appeared. Her lip was swollen and her hair stuck out at wild angles but she was intact. "Oh god, Isolde." She dropped to her knees.

"Not you too. Come on. Let's take her outside to my car." Lisbet didn't wait for an answer, she bent over and grabbed Isolde, throwing her over her shoulder. Blood dripped from her head onto the carpet.

"Fuck. *Fuck.* This is so fucked up." Beatrix stood, pulling Calla with her and the two of them followed Lisbet. Beatrix moved ahead, pulling the back door open and Lisbet shoved Isolde's lifeless body inside.

"I'll go with her. Bea, up front," Calla barked, pushing past the redhead and pulling the door shut behind her. The car lurched forward, and she remembered what a terrible driver Lisbet was, but there was no time.

"Isolde." She put a hand to her face, it was cold and clammy. She shook her shoulders. "Please." She could feel Beatrix's eyes on her. The silent question of if Isolde was okay. But Calla didn't know. She didn't know anything. A lifetime of fighting vampires and she didn't know shit about them.

She leaned closer, breathing in the metallic smell of blood. "Isolde, please." They turned onto the interstate just as police cars zipped by in the opposite direction, momentarily filling the car with blue and red light. "Please." Calla tried to brush Isolde's hair away from her face but it was thick with blood and pulled at her skin.

Isolde's eyes flicked open. "Calla." Her voice was hoarse.

"I'm here." She held Isolde's face in her hands, steadying herself against the bumping of the car with her legs. She almost asked what Isolde needed but wasn't it obvious? She didn't know much about vampires, but there was one thing she knew. "Here." She held her wrist to Isolde's mouth, it was filthy with soot. She could only imagine what she looked like.

"I can't." Isolde whispered, and from the front seat Beatrix let out a muffled sob.

"Yes." Calla wished they were alone, that she wasn't in the backseat of her best friend's car speeding down the interstate. She wished they had gotten their night. "You have my permission."

Isolde's eyes fluttered shut, and Beatrix made a strange gurgled sound. Calla grabbed her by the shoulders, shaking her. "You need blood. Drink, Isolde."

Her chest rose and fell, and then she lifted her hands and wrapped her fingers around Calla's wrist. The touch sent a shiver through her. She was doing this. She was letting a vampire feed from her.

Sharp teeth pierced her skin, but the pain was brief, replaced by a strange tingling feeling and then a pull. Calla closed her eyes, determined not to make any indecent noises. She could feel each beat of her heart, the blood pumping in her veins.. Warmth washed through her, heading straight between her legs.

Without realizing she had moved, she steadied herself with a hand on Isolde's hip as the vampire continued to feed. Calla opened her eyes to find the color returned to Isolde and the wound on her head stitching back together.

Pulling Calla closer, Isolde shifted her weight, pressing a knee between Calla's thighs and Calla let out a small groan. Lisbet cleared her throat, and Calla pulled back as Isolde dropped her wrist. Her bite marks closed immediately, leaving only red fang marks on her arm.

Calla knew she was blushing, her whole body felt on fire as Isolde pushed herself up, making a face as she felt the blood in her hair. "Thank you."

Calla nodded. "You're welcome." She wanted to be anywhere but in the car. She was nearly ready to open the door and hurl herself into traffic. What the fuck had just happened?

"Everybody okay?" Lisbet asked, taking a turn too sharply and Calla was thrown into Isolde's lap.

The vampire smirked and wrapped her arm around Calla's waist.

She glanced down at the hand on her ruined dress. She was going to smell like an ashtray for weeks. "Are you seriously flirting with me? You were dying like two minutes ago."

Isolde pressed her face in the crook of Calla's neck, her voice low. "You were delicious." She ran her hand lower onto Calla's leg and it took everything in her to not melt into the touch. Maybe she really should throw herself into traffic.

The car pulled into Isolde's driveway and Beatrix jumped out to punch the code into the gate. Calla used the opportunity to slide across the seat and press herself into the door. She kept her eyes on the back of Beatrix's headrest, but she could feel the heat of Isolde's stare on her neck.

Calla needed a cold shower and time to process what had just happened. She didn't think she was going to get either right away. Lisbet pulled in front of the house and everyone exited quickly. She headed for Isolde's door but Beatrix got there first and Lisbet blocked her path as she turned to go inside.

"Calla Chase."

"Lisbet Dupree."

Lisbet raised a perfectly groomed eyebrow. "You know I've always supported you and whoever you wanted to date—man, woman, neither, both. It's all been good to me. But a vampire, Calla? I mean, she's hot for sure, but that was…"

"She had to feed. She was dying, Lisbet." Yet Calla knew she was blushing again. Even her chest was red.

"You practically just boned in my backseat."

"Stop." Calla couldn't deal with this right now. "I almost got blown up. Can we do whatever this judgemental bullshit is later?"

Lisbet glanced down. "Shit." She raked her hand through her hair. "You're right. You're absolutely right." She grabbed Calla, pulling her into a bone-crushing hug. "I've missed you so much."

"I've missed you too." She pulled back. "What are we going to do?"

"I have no fucking idea, but we should probably go in and figure it out."

"Yes, but first I have got to clean up."

| Thirteen |

CALLA had never showered quicker in her life, though she wanted to stay under the hot water for the rest of her life. Scenes from the night kept flashing through her mind. The explosion. The bodies. Gus. Isolde's teeth sinking into her skin.

She turned off the water and stepped out, grabbing a towel and wrapping it around herself. She was thankful the hallway was empty, nothing had ever seemed more inviting than her bed waiting for her.

She pushed open the door and found Isolde, her hair dripping onto her silk robe on the other side. Calla clutched her towel tighter. "What are you doing here?"

"I live here." Isolde smiled and plopped herself down onto Calla's bed. The robe slipped open over her thighs. She was most definitely naked underneath.

"You almost died. You should rest." Calla pulled her eyes away from the hint of nipple underneath the red fabric and started across her room. Isolde was in front of her before she got three feet.

"I wanted to tell you thank you, again. For saving me. Twice."

Calla swallowed. A million scenarios ran through her head, most of them involving her pushing Isolde onto the bed behind her and ripping her robe off with her teeth. She was sure if she moved at all she'd do just that.

Isolde took another step towards Calla, pressing their bodies together. "I still want my night with you. I nearly died, but I've tasted you and that's all I can think of." Her hands were once again on Calla's hips, her leg between her thighs.

"We shouldn't," Calla said, though she made no attempt to stop Isolde. But Lisbet was below and the hunters had blown up the Vampire Human Alliance and despite what she wanted it was not the time. Still, she slipped her hand between the folds of Isolde's robe, running her thumb over the hardened peak of her breast. "Not now," she said, her voice weak.

"No?" Isolde tightened her grip on Calla, her fingers digging into her sides and the towel started to drop.

Calla withdrew her hands to grab it, bunching a handful in front of her chest. "No. We need a plan. Besides, I know Lisbet, and if I don't go back downstairs in the next five minutes she's going to be up here."

"Okay." Isolde raised her hands in surrender. "If that's what you want."

It most certainly wasn't what she wanted, but it was what she needed to do. "Yes. Time to get dressed." She stepped away and pulled open a dresser drawer. Before she could grab anything to wear, Isolde's hand darted out, grabbing a pair of running shorts. Calla spun around to find her shimmying them up underneath her robe. "You aren't even wearing underwear."

"Keep that in mind." Isolde winked. "What else do you have, little mortal?"

Was Isolde really wearing her clothes? The clothes she'd tried to make her get rid of? At least she was back to being irritated by the vampire. "Okay." She rummaged through the drawers and pulled out a crop-top she'd made from an oversized Titanic shirt. "Here." She held it out.

Isolde looked at the shirt, she looked back up at Calla. There was something in her eyes Calla didn't care for. Grinning, she shrugged off the robe, and it pooled on the floor beneath her feet and goddamn it, she was insanely hot. She pulled the shirt over her head, and Calla immediately realized her mistake at giving a woman with perfect tits and no bra a crop top to wear.

"How do I look?"

Calla made a grunting noise. She looked fantastic. She always did. "Good, I guess. I need to get dressed." Isolde resumed sitting on the bed. She should ask her to leave. She should not change in front of the vampire she just let feed from her. She let her towel drop. "How do I look?"

"Fuck your friends and those murderous hunters. *Please.* Come here."

Calla turned around, grabbing a pair of underwear and pulled them on. She was going to blame the explosion for every choice she was making. Certainly she was concussed or in shock. "Beg again." She pulled on her shorts and turned around. She was not expecting to find the vampire on her knees.

"Like this?"

And Calla would have given in but there was a knock on the door. "What are you doing? Did you drown in the shower?" Lisbet asked.

Smirking, Isolde popped up. "Be right out."

Calla shot her a look, put on the nearest shirt and jerked the door open. Lisbet's eyes slid past Calla and to the vampire behind her shoulder. Calla knew exactly what she was seeing, Isolde, hair still wet, in Calla's clothes. "Really?"

"She..."

"Well, times a wastin'" Isolde shouldered her way past both of them.

Lisbet frowned and took a deep breath. "Calla Eugenia Chase, I know she's very hot and spooky, and you've always been into dangerous things but *right now*? Really?"

"I'm not the horny one. She is. It's the blood," Calla hissed, fairly certain Isolde would hear her anyway. "It's over. Move along." She walked past her.

Lisbet followed, whispering—or rather, quietly screeching—in Calla's ear, "Oh, we're discussing this later. We are most definitely discussing how the fucking queen of the vampires just came out of your room in your clothes. In the birthday Titanic shirt I gave you, no less. For shame, Calla. What would Kate Winslet think? For shame."

At the bottom of the steps, she heard Molly's voice but couldn't make out the words. Then Isolde laughed.

"Are you done?" Calla put a hand on her hip. "There was an explosion. Are you really going to waste our time like this?" Calla could barely contain her smile.

"Mmhmm. Vampire fucker." Lisbet grabbed her arm and pulled her down the stairs. "I can't believe you left me alone in this haunted house."

As they descended, shame and horror latched their oily fingers into Calla's gut. Then anger flared as she stepped into the room with Beatrix and Isolde. Gus had blown up a building she was in. He'd set off a bomb. He'd killed people, he'd almost killed Isolde.

Calla sat down, as far away from Isolde as she could get. "So..."

"So your old friends declared war," Isolde said, opening a cabinet and revealing a TV. So she did own one, even if it was the smallest TV Calla had ever seen. Photos flashed across the screen as reporters talked about the carnage. Calla had known it was bad, but she'd been focused on finding Isolde. Five people were dead, including the Congressman. Another two dozen were injured.

"What do we do?" Calla asked because she truly had no idea. She was a fighter, a soldier. This was well beyond anything she was prepared for.

Before anyone could answer there was a knock on the door. Isolde stood up. "I'll get it." She pulled back her shoulders.

"Don't worry, I think I know who it is," Lisbet said, looking at Calla. "I found something out right before I showed up. It's... well, you'll see."

Hope swelled in Calla, but she tried to hold it at bay until she got to the door. Her mother was standing on the other side. Delphine was thinner than she usually was, her hair was frizzy, but she was whole. "Mama?"

"Baby." Delphine threw her arms around Calla, and she melted into her mother's embrace.

"How?" She asked when they finally pulled apart.

"Before their little excursion, Gus managed to get me out."

"No." Calla stepped back from her mother, shaking her head. "No. No."

"Calla, wait." Delphine put up her hands. "I had no part in that. I didn't know. I would never put you in danger. Never. I'm not on his side."

"And I'm supposed to believe you're on ours?" Isolde said from behind Calla. "Why are you at my home?"

Delphine straightened and the pounds she had lost no longer mattered. She was still a warrior. "Because you kidnapped my daughter, you sneaky—" She trailed off as her eyes caught on Isolde's clothes.

"Wait." Calla put her arms out, standing between her mother and Isolde. "Mom, there's a whole lot you've missed. We're... I don't know. I think we're on the same side. At the very least everyone in this house agrees we shouldn't be blowing each other up."

"I came to get you," Delphine said, her hand on her hip. The outline of a stake was visible beneath her shirt.

"A moment." Calla tried to convey everything she wanted to say to Isolde through her eyes, but she didn't think it worked. She stepped out of the house and pulled the door shut, hauling her mother further down the porch. It wouldn't be long before the sun came up. "Mom, listen."

"Calla, what have you done?"

"What have I done? I tried to save you! Are you kidding? What have I done? What is the Council doing? Split in half? Blowing people up? Did you know how many lies they told us?" Tears welled in her eyes and she wiped them away before they could fall.

"I did not not." Delphine said, glancing up at the gargoyle above her head. Calla recognized the look on her mother's face. She always got it when she was thinking about something she'd rather not. "Do you trust her?"

"I'm starting to."

"Okay." Delphine nodded. "Do you love her?"

"What?" Calla sputtered, taking a step back. "Love her? Because she's wearing my shirt? That's... that was a little joke. She thinks she's funny."

The door swung open, and Calla was certain Isolde had heard their entire conversation. "Okay, enough." She motioned them both inside. When neither of them moved, she pushed the door open further with her foot. "Delphine, let me jog your memory. First, you murdered a dear friend of mine, so quit looking at me like I'm the bad guy. Second, some of your little friends tried to kill me *and* your daughter, so whatever you're thinking about me you can just squash it down for now. And if you're trying to get her to leave, you can fuck right off and leave my property because you aren't taking Calla anywhere."

"Isolde..."

"No." She turned towards Calla and the icy stare she had sent at Delphine melted. She took Calla's hands in her own. "You're safe here. Beatrix has called in extra security. Don't leave. *Please.*"

"Calla, We need to get out of here," Delphine said.

Isolde spun towards her. "You can stay or you can go, but you're taking Calla over my dead body."

"That can be arranged." Delphine pulled the stake from her waistband.

"Stop!" Calla yelled. "I'm staying, mom. And I'd like you to stay too, because she's right. We're safer here than out there. But I can't do this. I know you were just locked up, and I know you've been having a worse time than me, but I almost died. Isolde almost died and you're either going to stop or you're going to leave."

"Maybe we all need to rest," Lisbet offered, as she came out onto the porch. "It's 4 a.m. We're all tired. Isolde nearly died. But I think we're all, mostly, on the same side. That side being not doing any mass murders. So, maybe a rest?"

"Are you asking to spend the night?" Isolde asked, the bite out of her voice. "Because yes, that would be fine."

"Thank you," Lisbet said. "Delphine? Retract the claws, please. It wasn't a vampire that tried to murder your kid today."

"Okay." She shoved the stake into her pocket. "A truce."

Isolde nodded. "Yes. I've heard this from a Chase before. Beatrix will show you to your room. Lisbet is right, I need to rest." She started back towards the house and Calla didn't even think before she let her fingers brush against Isolde's. Before she grabbed them and squeezed. She let go quickly and none of the others seemed to notice. But Isolde sucked in a breath.

| Fourteen |

WHEN Calla opened the doors to her bedroom she was surprised, and a little disappointed, that Isolde wasn't there. Instead, there was a letter waiting for her in the middle of her bed, a long stemmed rose laid on top.

My room?

This was a bad idea. Possibly a terrible idea. But she was back in the hallway. Calla had never been in Isolde's room but she knew where it was. She hurried across the rug lined hallways on bare feet until she stood outside of her door. She hesitated. Then she knocked.

A moment passed then the door was open and Isolde was pulling her inside. Her room was full of trinkets from different centuries, furs were draped over nearly every surface including a massive four-poster bed. And in the middle of the room was Isolde, still in her stupid Titanic shirt.

"I can't believe you're still wearing that."

"It smells like you."

And that was all it took. Calla grabbed Isolde, fisting a handful of her hair, and pulling her into a desperate kiss. Isolde moaned into her mouth, her tongue parting Calla's lips. She pulled Calla close with one hand, the other making its way under her shirt.

"Vampires are strong right?" Calla said, but instead of an answer Isolde caught Calla's lip between her teeth. It was all the answer she needed to wrap her legs around Isolde's waist and they stumbled back, landing on the bed.

And Isolde was strong. She flipped Calla over, as she had so many times, and pinned her hands above her head. "You're so beautiful."

Though she shouldn't, Calla knew what she wanted, or at least one of the things she wanted. The dark, dangerous thing she'd never let herself think about before. "Bite me again." She arched her neck, savoring the way Isolde's eyes followed it. The way they flashed with desire.

The vampire lowered her head, but her teeth only grazed Calla's neck before being replaced by her lips. One hand moved down her stomach and beneath the waistband of her shorts. "You must be sure," Isolde whispered, her words moving down Calla's spine and making her toes curl.

She would never be sure. All of this felt like a dream but one she did not want to end. She could spend her life in this bed, Isolde's fingers working between her legs, forgetting the rest of the world. "Must I?"

"Perhaps I wish you to be the one to beg this time, mortal." The hand between her legs retreated. Her splayed fingers moved slowly up Calla until they were at her throat. She pushed her chin to the side. "What do you want?"

"You." Calla trembled.

Teeth sunk into Calla's neck and her back lifted off the bed, before she crashed back down. The world narrowed to a pinprick where Isolde's mouth touched her skin. She grabbed a handful of the sheets beneath her, moaning Isolde's name.

The vampire took Calla's hand, placing it between her legs. She was slick and warm and it only took a few brushes of Calla's fingers before she jerked against her. She was everything Calla had spent her whole life looking for. They pressed their bodies together and Calla pushed her fingers inside of Isolde while her thumb continued to circle. "There?" The vampire moaned and Calla pressed harder.

As she did, Isolde deepened the bite, shuddering as she came around Calla's fingers buried inside her. Heat rushed to Calla's core, spiraling deep into her. With a final brush of her thumb, she pulled her fingers away.

Groaning with pleasure, Isolde brought her head up, blood dripping down the corner of her mouth. Then she was kissing Calla again, and instead of blood it was magic sparking against her tongue as Isolde removed her clothes with expert fingers.

She wanted to move, to touch every inch of Isolde but her limbs were heavy. Isolde trailed kisses down her chest, between her breasts, lower to her stomach and then to her center. Isolde's tongue darted out, the briefest pressure on her clit.

"Are you too tired to cum, sweet mortal?"

Truthfully, she could barely keep her eyes open but did not want this to end. "Please," she whispered, and the vampire licked her again. This time harder. And Isolde had told the truth when she said she knew so many things. Or maybe Calla had already been close. Maybe she had been waiting for this moment. She ran her hands through Isolde's hair, and the vampire reached up, brushing her fingers across the spot on Calla's neck where she had sunk her teeth.

Calla exploded, she screamed, back arching. Isolde held firm, bringing her slowly down, until Calla was panting. She glanced up from between her legs and kissed her thighs "One day, I will bite here. So close. The perfect vein. But tonight it is late."

Calla couldn't seem to make her tongue work. "Mmm." Was all she could manage. Then she realized what she had done. The vampire had fed from her twice tonight. She was human. There was only so much blood in her body.

"Easy," Isolde said, pressing her hand against Calla's chest, right above her heart. "You are frightened?"

"I'm lightheaded."

"Of course." Isolde crawled back up her body. "You need blood." She brought her wrist to her mouth.

"Will it?"

"Turn you? I would have to drain you. You would have to die. This is just... it is what we do, Calla. You have wondered why the mortals feed us—"

Calla managed to turn onto her side. "I have fewer questions now."

"You will have even less after you drink. And no arguing. You must. I should not have gotten so carried away." She bit her wrist and brought it to Calla's mouth.

Calla hesitated. She didn't have a medical degree, but she was fairly certain the best way to do blood transfusions was not via mouth. However, Isolde had been a vampire for nearly a millennia and had somehow, in less than ten minutes, given her the best orgasm of her life. Which wasn't really a medical skill, but it somehow seemed relevant.

She brought Isolde's wrist to her mouth and the magic she had tasted before filled her. It was indescribable, floating, growing pleasure, pure happiness. Desire.

Isolde slipped her leg between Calla's thigh and she pressed into her as she drank.

When she was done, she was not sure she would ever catch her breath. She stared at the ceiling. Isolde was at her side and she slid her hand down, intertwining their fingers. "I am sorry for today. I had better plans for our first time."

"You did?" Calla looked over at her. She was flushed, something Calla rarely saw on her pale face. Her golden hair pooled around her on the bed, her brown eyes were dark and deep. And she was timeless. Calla did not think there had been a moment in her long life where Isolde was not the most beautiful woman in the world.

She smiled. "Of course. Naturally, anything would be better than almost dying and then fucking you while I know your mother is on the floor below, but I was going to have flowers. Petals scattered. I would take you to your room, remove your clothes, piece by piece. I would put you on the desk, get on my knees and not stop until the sun rose."

"No biting?"

"No. I did not plan to drink from you." She brushed a piece of Calla's hair behind her ear. "I love your hair, some of it is brown but these highlights are like honey." She moved her hand to Calla's cheek. "And your eyes. Big and blue, as though you might be innocent if I did not know better."

Calla kissed her. "Isolde?"

"Hmm?"

"I very much liked the biting."

When Calla opened her eyes, it took a moment for her to remember where she was, bundled under furs, the mid afternoon sun barely penetrating thick curtains. Then, the woman beside her moved, pressing her naked body into Calla's and throwing an arm over her chest.

Calla froze. She'd slept with a vampire. Willingly. *Very* willingly. And that was hardly the worst, or biggest, thing that had happened yesterday. Somewhere in the same house was her mother and Lisbet. Somewhere beyond that was Gus, who had tried to kill her.

She let her gaze linger on Isolde. Though she was softer in sleep, her features were still sharp, her lips red. Her color was better than Calla had ever seen it. She looked human, innocent and sweet.

No wonder the Council had always told them to kill a vampire on sight. She still understood it. They weren't all like Isolde; they killed people and many of their victims were very unwilling. Were vampires just like people? Were some good and some bad? But even Isolde had killed. She'd spoken of her overwhelming blood lust when she was young.

Isolde opened her eyes, blinking slowly, and then a grin spread across her face, lighting her eyes. "Good morning."

Calla wanted to return the sentiment. She'd never woken up next to a more beautiful woman, next to someone who pushed all her buttons in the most delicious way, but another part of her wanted to scream, to flee. To go cry to Lisbet about the terrible thing she'd done.

The smile fell from Isolde's face. "You are full of regret."

"No," Calla said, and she wasn't sure if she was lying. "Just thinking about all the other things that happened yesterday." She ran her knuckles against Isolde's cheek and it sent a thrill through her. Mistake or not, she wasn't sure she'd be able to stop. Being around Isolde was addictive.

"We will find a solution. I promise." Isolde pulled her closer and kissed her softly. "In all my years, I have learned that there is always a way forward. One way or another, you eventually come out on the other side."

Calla sighed and laid back against her pillow. "Right now I don't even know what the other side is. What does it look like?"

Isolde put her head on Calla's chest and traced patterns on her bare stomach. "Then that is what we will do first. We will eventually go downstairs and find the others, then we will decide, together, what the future looks like."

"I'm not sure my mother will be a great ally." Calla held Isolde, wishing she could capture this moment; the pressure of Isolde on her chest, the way her hair tickled Calla's skin. "She hates vampires."

"As do you." Isolde trailed her fingers lower, running them across Calla's thighs.

Did she hate vampires? Part of Calla did, even as she let one stroke her, keep her locked away as a plaything. Innocent people died at their hands. But innocent people had died at Gus's hands yesterday and he was a human. "How many vampires *want* to move forward towards a peaceful existence?"

Isolde stilled her hands. "Not all of them, Calla. Not nearly all of them."

Calla had never seen herself as a leader, had never desired the spotlight, but she had always seen herself as a protector. She had been little more than a child when she had first understood the weight of sacrifice, but she had never shied from it. She had always been ready to protect others. "So, we need to gather the ones who want what we want. It will be the same as it always is, those who are good, who care about others, versus those who don't."

Someone knocked on the door. "Mistress?" It was Beatrix on the other side. "There is someone for you at the door."

"Someone else?" Isolde pulled away from Calla, leaving her cold. "It seems everyone is already here."

"Biyu is here. May I let her in?"

Isolde rose from the bed, naked and perfect. "Yes, of course. I will be down in a moment."

"Okay." Beatrix's voice wavered. "Please hurry. The others are already up." Her footsteps sounded down the hall as she left.

Calla stood, reaching for her discarded clothing. "Time to enact that plan."

Isolde grinned. "It seems so."

| Fifteen |

BY the time Calla made it downstairs less than ten minutes later, the parlor felt more like a war zone. Biyu was sitting, her long hair in a knot on top of her head, watching Delphine pace the room. Lisbet was alert, perched in a chair across from Biyu, a cup of steaming coffee in her hand.

"Nice of you to join us," Delphine said, eyeing Calla.

"Good morning, mother." She kissed her cheek and glanced at Lisbet. She was sure her best friend would have plenty to say, and she'd rather hear that than whatever her mother was going to scream the second they were alone together. If she even held it together until they were alone. Delphine's gaze darted between Biyu and Isolde, clearly struggling to not pounce on either of the vampires.

"I have invited Ezra. He will be here tonight," Biyu said, delicately lifting a cup of tea off the side table and sipping it. "I am sure he will have useful suggestions."

"Well, nothing like uninvited guests inviting more guests," Isolde said.

"Oh, hush." Biyu waved her hand dismissively and Calla couldn't help but like the vampire at least a little bit. However, the house was filling up, and though it was large, the make-up of people and volatile personalities was making it seem small.

Isolde must have been thinking the same thing. "I am beginning to feel as though I run a halfway house."

"Haven't you always?" Biyu said, which Calla didn't understand but made a mental note to ask about later.

"Calla, a word." Lisbet nodded towards the hallway.

Calla looked between her mother and the two vampires. Leaving them together didn't seem like a safe move. "Listen,"—she cleared her throat—"No murder. No violence. We all want to keep people safe. Isolde and I were talking this morning and we believe there is a way for us to all work together."

That was the wrong thing to say. "Oh, does your fanged lover think so? Honestly, Calla." Delphine stopped her pacing and Biyu started to push up from her chair, but Isolde stopped her with a shake of her head.

Calla walked to her mother and put her hands on her shoulders. There were bags under her eyes, and anger running through them. Calla wished she could soothe her hurt the way her mother had soothed her so many times. She lowered her voice though she knew the others could still hear. "Mom, the Council betrayed us. They imprisoned you."

"She imprisoned you, Calla," Delphine said.

"I know. But she's a prisoner too." Calla glanced back at Isolde to find Biyu looking up at her, the same way Lisbet was staring at Calla. "And right now, we've got to work together. We've got to come up with a plan. And stop arguing. As we established last night, everyone is free to leave. If you'd rather walk out and be blown up, or attacked or whatever the fuck else is waiting for us, go ahead, otherwise shut up. Respectfully."

"I like her," Biyu said. "She was the perfect choice."

"I just... I need a moment," Lisbet said. She was clenching her jaw so tightly Calla worried she would break something. "Do you have... I need a drink."

"It's not even two," Calla said.

"Yes," Isolde said. "Let me show you. Then I'll leave you alone to drink."

Lisbet's jaw twitched. "Okay."

"I can point out the safe boundaries if you need a walk." Isolde caught Calla's eye as she was leaving the room and winked.

Gratitude filled Calla, and she let herself relax slightly. Isolde was charming when she wanted to be. There was hope they could all find a way to work together.

"I need a moment too," Delphine said, squeezing Calla's shoulder as she left and Calla watched her leave.

"Well, sweet human, we have been left alone." Biyu crossed one leg over the other. "Sit." She patted the seat next to her. "How was it when you first moved in? Was Isolde as overbearing as when I was turned."

Calla slid into the seat. "She turned you?"

"Oh, heavens no. Isolde has never turned anyone. She absolutely refuses. But my sire was killed shortly after I was made, and she took me in. She loves taking people in, though she won't admit it, but then she wants to make them little Isoldes." Biyu lowered her voice. "I don't think she's ever properly learned to make friends. She's learned some skills over the years, but Isolde is terrible with people."

"That can't be true," Calla said. "She seduced a king."

"Being very beautiful is not the same as being very charming, but men often can't tell the difference." She looked Calla up and down. "You must be hungry. Come on." She stood and offered her hand. Calla accepted. Though Biyu was small, she was strong.

Calla followed her towards the kitchen. "Are you going to stay here?"

"For a time. Isolde had the last of the witches charm the estate. It is as safe a place as you can find in times of trouble." She slowed her stride to match pace with Calla. "You were a good choice for a human mouthpiece, though I think the Directorate will have to change its mission for her after the explosion."

"Yeah, but you only have so much time."

"So they say." Biyu held the kitchen door open for Calla.

A woman Calla had only seen in passing was inside frying a pan of bacon. She pulled a plate from the cabinets and greeted them. "I made plenty, do you want some?"

"That would be incredible. I'm starving," Calla said, walking around the counter.

"Now, as for what happened yesterday," Biyu continued their conversation,, "I think it will both help and hurt our chances. Most humans will be outraged, especially publicly. Bombs are never a good look. But some will secretly agree."

Calla grabbed the plate the woman prepared for her, thanking her. She leaned close to Biyu, hoping she couldn't be heard over the sizzling of the bacon. "Yeah, but the hourglass. You'll die."

"What?" Biyu rummaged in the fridge and came up with a bottle of thick red liquid. "The hourglass?"

Calla's mouth went dry. She'd suspected it was a lie, at least the heart of it, but Biyu didn't even know what she was talking about. And she knew that Isolde had been given a mission. Had the Directorate simply not told Biyu or was the hourglass something else entirely?

"Dining room," Biyu said, glancing at the cook and leaving the kitchen quickly.

The dining room made Calla think of her first days in the house, sitting defiantly in her underwear across from Isolde. Now she felt the same defiance rise in her. What was Isolde hiding?

Biyu ran her fingers over the silver candelabras on the table. "Oh, Isolde, you strange little bird," she muttered and then turned to Calla. "But the bird did not grow old by squawking all its secrets across the world. Now, what is this about an hourglass?"

"You just told me not to squawk my secrets." Calla folded her arms across her chest. The room danced with the light from the chandelier above. The two stared at each other, Biyu seemingly not needing to blink.

Mustering her courage and unsure if the vampire would pounce on her the moment she left the room, Calla turned on her heel and walked out. The house was still a labyrinth, but she was getting better at navigating its halls. She turned down one, then another until she was at the library.

Calla wasn't sure what had drawn her there, how she had known she would find Isolde, but moments later she came into view, curled up in a chair, pulp fiction with a steamy cover held in front of her face.

"Isolde."

She shoved the book beside her, into the folds of the chair. "What?"

A quip was on her tongue, but before she could speak, Calla lost her nerve. She wasn't sure she wanted to know all of Isolde's secrets. She already had so many regrets. She sat in the chair across from Isolde, sinking into the thick cushions. "You're lying to me."

Isolde said nothing, only sat up straighter. Her face gave nothing away.

"I mentioned the hourglass to Biyu and—"

"Why would you do that?" Isolde sprang from her seat. "You petulant child! Are you trying to destroy me?"

Calla stood back up. "Excuse me?" Her chest tightened and her body vibrated with frustration. She had given Isolde everything she wanted. She had given the vampire her blood, her body, she had cared for her. What Calla didn't want to acknowledge was the embarrassment she felt, how easily she had spoken to Biyu, assuming that because Isolde had seemed to like her she could trust her. She knew better than that. They were still vampires, and she had let all her training fall to the side.

"You weren't even supposed to see it, and now you think you are owed an explanation? Why, because we spent the night together? If I spilled every secret to my lovers, my mouth would never close, much like yours."

Calla shook her head wishing she could erase the last five minutes. She clenched her fists at her side and Isolde glanced down at them. The vampire smirked. "Will you hit me again, mortal?"

Calla wanted to. She could picture her heart, sitting just off center in her chest. There were tables, chairs, plenty of wood in this room. But Isolde wanted that, wanted Calla to swing and wrestle and forget the reason she had come into the room when Isolde sat on top of her, chest heaving. "Tell me the truth. You want us to work together, then stop lying to me. Or I'll leave."

"You won't leave."

"I will. And then you will be left alone to deal with the Directorate."

"We are both hunted, Calla. Do not pretend it is only me." She took a step closer, her body tense, her eyes narrowed, and took Calla's hand. "You will stay. You will sleep in my bed again, and you will keep your mouth shut, and we will do as we said. We'll work together."

"You have forgotten who I am, Isolde. You've trapped me in this house and collared me, and like an idiot I've sat and stayed and heeled like an obedient dog, but I'm a hunter. I have killed countless vampires. Every fight we had I've held back. But I'm not Beatrix. I won't follow you blindly."

"Calla…" Isolde swallowed hard.

The library seemed cavernous, each moment stretching out, thinning the air. Though the house was full of people making noise around them, Calla could not take her eyes or thoughts from Isolde and all the tumultuous feelings inside her, rattling around. She wanted to do as she said, she wanted to lay in bed with a vampire between her legs and forget about everything else. She wanted, for once, to take the easy path. But she could not.

"I have to leave."

Rage twisted Isolde's features, and she struck out, knocking books off of a nearby table. They went flying into the stacks and paper rained down on them. "You followed every order those hunter bastards gave you. You spew lies at me because you know the truth, you already admitted to it. You have been nothing but an obedient, unthinking dog your entire life. And all I ask for is trust, for a moment of belief in me, and you would walk away?"

Calla reeled, the words striking her worse than any fist. She turned, but the fury inside of her grew. She smashed her palms into a shelf and it went down. The books crashed to the floor, an antique globe shattered, and Isolde launched herself at Calla.

But Calla was faster. She caught Isolde and flung her away with all the force she could muster. Isolde crashed into the empty table and it shattered beneath her, leaving her in a pile of wood.

"You useless mutt," Isolde snarled. "I should never have dragged you from obscurity. I should have left you alone, you could have fallen into the bed of that worthless little Council member just as easily as mine and saved yourself so much trouble."

Calla walked closer. "Vampire. Blood sucker. *Murderer.*" She repeated the words in her head. Vampires were beautiful and alluring, but they were heartless killers. She had let herself forget. Had let herself get swept up. But there was no reason for humans to accept vampires. They should be wiped off the face of the earth. And maybe it would sting, maybe sometimes at night she would think of Isolde and her fangs in her neck, but she would be gone, dust and ash, and Calla would be free.

She could live the life she always wanted. She would not have to hunt anymore. She could go to school. She could get a job. She could have a future. She put a foot on Isolde's chest and bent over, picking up a piece of wood, its point sharp.

Isolde's eyes went wide, staring at the stake in Calla's hand. She tried to push herself up but Calla dropped her weight onto her, trapping the vampire against the pile of wood. It was just one movement of her arm. One quick motion and Isolde would be gone.

Tears welled in Isolde's eyes. "Calla." She wrapped her fingers around Calla's wrist. "Don't do this. Please. Don't do this."

All she had to do was move her arm. She knew how it would feel, how the wood would hit resistance and still drive lower. How it would squelch, and then the resistance would be gone and so would all her troubles.

But her arm did not move.

"I'll die, Calla! I know you are angry with me, but I will die!" The tears fell from Isolde's eyes, splattering across her cheeks and wetting her eyelashes.

The stake fell from Calla's hands. She pushed herself up. "We're done," she said.

Isolde was on her knees, the tears still falling. "Calla, wait." Her fingers brushed Calla's ankles. "I'm sorry. I didn't mean it. Please."

Calla kept walking through the half destroyed library. All she had to do was find her mother and Lisbet, and they would be done. The sun was up, Isolde could not follow. And though she might leave behind a part of her heart, Calla would be free. She was done fighting, done with all of this. She did not need a solution. She did not need a way forward. She needed to disappear. To become someone else.

Vampire problems were not her problems and after the explosion neither were the hunters.

None of it mattered. That's what she told herself as she hurried through the estate. That was her old life, and she was starting a new one. When Biyu tried to stop her, concern on her face, Calla only shook her off. She didn't know enough to try harder.

Once, right before she found her mother she thought she heard Isolde's cries from somewhere above but she did not stop to listen. Her heart had always been a fool.

| Sixteen |

"CALLA, what the hell." Lisbet had said the same thing at least half a dozen times since they'd left Isolde's estate.

Calla's cheek pressed against the glass of the window. Every few minutes her mother's hand would reach from the back, stroking her hair before retreating. Trees and billboards zipped past but Calla barely noticed them. All she could see was Isolde's face below her, tears streaming down her face. She flexed her fingers, remembering the feeling of the wood in her hand.

"I'm sorry," she murmured, the noise of the car swallowing her words.

Lisbet glanced away from the road and at Calla. "You look like shit." She sighed. "We need some kind of plan. What are we doing?"

"Nothing," Calla said, firmer this time. "I mean, I can't stop you all, but I'm doing nothing. I'm done. Completely done. I'm done with vampires. I'm done with the Council. I'm *done*."

Silence bloomed in the car, full of unsaid things. Delphine was the first to break it. "Me too. I'm sorry girls. I'm sorry I never stood up for the things in the Council I knew were wrong, and I'm sorry for killing that vampire and getting you so caught up in my mess."

"Then I'm out too," Lisbet said. "And it's totally fine how you abandoned the vampire after you spent the night with her and told us all we were going to work together. Seriously, no complaints. But what, exactly, are we going to do?"

Calla's breath fogged the glass. "Get away from here."

"Cool. Cool. But do you have any money?" Lisbet slowed the car and pulled over to the side of the road. "I'm really not trying to be a pain, it's just...I have like five hundred dollars in my bank account right now and all my clothes are in my trunk. The Council paid for everything for us."

"Hand me that." Calla pointed to one of the bags in the back seat and her mother handed it over. She got out of the car and rummaged around for a moment to find one of Isolde's necklaces. "I took this with me. It's got to be worth something." The diamonds glittered in the sun.

Calla had missed the sun.

And she definitely, totally didn't miss Isolde. She definitely didn't hate herself for the way Isolde had looked—terrified and crying.

No. She'd made the right choice. The Council may not have been perfect but vampires were monsters. Calla could *not* love a vampire, and she wouldn't let herself go any further down that path.

Her mother paced behind her, kicking up dirt on the side of the road. "It is, but we'll have to take it to a pawnshop and even a few thousand isn't going to last us that long," she said then noticed the look on Calla's face. "But it's okay. We're going to be okay. I've been a waitress, I can do it again."

Calla leaned against the cool metal of the car. The trees were bare, and she felt exposed though the road was deserted. "I've got some cash on me. Let's just get a hotel room for tonight." She almost apologized again, but she knew they'd just assure her that everything was fine.

Nothing was fine.

She reached into her pocket and considered pulling out her phone, but she knew what she would find—an almost unending stream of texts from Beatrix and nothing from Isolde. Why did she keep checking?

You have been nothing but an obedient, unthinking dog your entire life.

The rage she had felt in that moment had seeped away and made room for sadness. She made her way back into the once again silent car. They were all too antsy to sit for long, but they needed to move, get away from the city, find somewhere without a hunters headquarters, somewhere beyond the Council and vampires and all the shit that had consumed Calla's life.

What Calla really wanted was a pint of ice cream, a cheesy movie marathon and time to cry, because for everything she had told herself, all the lies she had tried to cram into her mind, she knew what she felt was heartbreak.

Her mother was asleep on one of the queen beds that made up the dingy motel room they had rented for the night. Lisbet was deep into her phone. She hadn't looked up more than twice in the last half hour. Calla murmured something about needing air, Lisbet nodded, and she slipped outside, alone for the first time all day.

They weren't far from New Dunwich, but Calla had never been to the town they had stopped in before. Some tiny place with one stoplight and a grocery store that smelled like cleaner with a side of rotten meat.

The parking lot was almost deserted and the light above the office flickered like the beginning of a horror movie. Calla walked behind the motel towards the open field that looked like someone had once started to build something and given up after a few days. She'd managed to sweet talk a quarter of a bottle of vodka from the desk clerk, who had called her "even sadder than the usual crowd" on the way in.

She found a soft-looking patch of ground, took a long and disgusting drink, and laid down, staring up at the crescent moon. Her life had been simmering for a while but she'd fully blown it up.

And she hated how much it hurt. She wanted to hate Isolde. When she agreed to her plan, she was certain she would. Isolde was pretentious and frustrating and overbearing. She was all the things Calla couldn't stand. She was nothing like the people Calla had dated before.

She sat halfway up, and tried to take another swallow of the worst vodka she'd ever tasted, but poured most of it down the front of her shirt. She cursed loudly. Her words echoed through the field and off the cinder block motel.

"Keep it up and you'll wake up one of the terrifying residents of this establishment," Lisbet said, emerging from the shadows. She sat beside Calla and stuck her hand out for the bottle. "Absolutely vile," she said after tasting it. "Feels appropriate."

"I fucked it up."

"Oh, you idiot. Everybody fucked it up. I don't know why you're putting this all on yourself. The vampires fucked it up, the hunters fucked

160

it up, the humans fucked it up. I really don't think this whole transition could have gone much worse." Lisbet laid on the ground beside Calla, crossing her arms behind her head. "Unless you're talking about something else."

"I can't *like* a vampire, Lisbet. I'm not even sure I do. She's the most annoying person I have ever met."

"Oh, come on. You've met Gus."

Calla started to chuckle, but it died in her throat. "He tried to kill me. He knew I was there. He spoke to me. And he still blew it up. All those innocent people…"

"And that's why you have to let some of that guilt go." Lisbet's hand found Calla's and she intertwined their fingers. "This is so much bigger than you."

"What if my guilt is about something else?" Calla said, forcing the words out before she could second guess herself.

"Well, that would be okay too." Lisbet sat up and Calla did the same. The two women stared at each other, though Calla could barely make out any of her best friend's details in the dark night, except her black hair brushing her shoulders, highlighted silver by the moon. "What happened? *How* did it happen?"

Calla shrugged, taking another drink. "I don't know. I really don't. I keep trying to think of a moment, *the moment*, you know? But there were just a lot of small ones, when she wasn't Isolde, cold and collected vampire, but the woman Isolde, still full of humanity underneath it all."

"I think I was there for the big one, C. The way you looked when you thought she was dying. It was the look of someone in—"

"Don't say it. I can't hear it."

"Okay." Lisbet settled deeper into the grass, her feet out in front of her. Around them crickets chirped and a car drove by, its headlights briefly illuminating the road before disappearing. "I'm scared, Calla. I know your mom was talking about waitressing, but I have no skills besides fighting."

"Me either," Calla said, glad to be thinking of something else. "We could be muscle for hire."

"You're joking but I've thought about it. I could be a bodyguard." Lisbet yawned and then wrapped her arm around Calla's shoulder. "I'm exhausted, I could barely sleep in that creepy vampire mansion last night, but I couldn't leave you alone out here. You ready for bed?"

"Yeah." Calla stood up, pulling Lisbet with her. "Thanks, you know, for not letting me sit out here alone."

"Of course. For all we know werewolves are coming out next and I can't have you eaten."

"It's a half-moon," Calla pointed out, starting back towards the motel.

"The full moon thing could have been a ruse."

| Seventeen |

DELPHINE was a flurry of movement, haphazardly shoving the few belongings they had with them into a duffle bag. "Let's just get to the coast."

"It's winter, mother." Calla looked around the room again, making sure they weren't leaving anything behind. She patted her pocket to make sure the necklace was still there. First stop, pawnshop.

"I didn't say the beach." She zipped up the duffle and slung it across the room. It landed with a thud near the door. Some things never changed and Calla's mother being a hurricane of a human being was one of them. Delphine had always been wild, even in Calla's earliest memories. She'd gotten pregnant at nineteen by a man Calla had never met, and it had barely slowed her down.

Calla's first memories were of sitting in the Council headquarters watching her mother train, amazed by the way she would make people fly across the room. She seemed like magic. Calla had squeezed her eyes shut and begged whoever was listening that she would get the hunter genes, that she wouldn't be stuck on the Council unable to truly fight. At nine she'd realized she had them and nearly wept with joy.

"Okay, fine. We'll head for the coast." It might do Calla some good to smell the salty air, to dip her toes in the freezing Atlantic.

"Oh, I love the beach," Lisbet said, emerging from the bathroom. The smell of cheap lavender soap came with her.

Someone knocked on the door, and all three of them froze, slowly turning towards the noise.

Not Isolde. Please don't let it be Isolde. It had only been a day. Calla couldn't see her yet. She didn't have it in her.

"Calla!" It was Beatrix's voice, and Calla wasn't sure if she was relieved or not.

She pulled open the door and stepped outside. "How did you find us?"

Beatrix looked like hell. Her red hair was pulled on top of her head and even calling it a messy bun would be generous. Dark bags—worsened by smeared mascara—under her eyes gave away how little she must have slept. A bolt of guilt zapped through Calla. She hadn't considered what her leaving might mean for the others. How Isolde might rage.

"I have my ways," Beatrix said, walking away from the motel and into the parking lot.

Calla followed her over the pavement and towards a bit of grass that separated the motel from the road. All the landscaping was dead, and Calla couldn't tell if it was from the winter weather or lack of care. Beatrix was looking at her, waiting for her to say something, but Calla wasn't going to be the one to give in. She had followed Calla across state lines, she could open the conversation.

"Why?" She finally asked. Her feet were planted firmly, her hands lightly balled, as though she were ready to fight.

"I was a prisoner, Beatrix."

"That's a lie." Beatrix stepped closer. "You've *been* a prisoner. That isn't why you left and she won't say. I've never seen her so distraught."

The words Calla wanted to say wouldn't come out. Isolde was distraught? She'd expected her to be angry, raging even. But sad? Calla shook out her hands. That didn't matter. She could cry and gnash her teeth, but Calla had to leave. If she didn't, that would be her life. She would fall in love with a vampire.

She would fall in love with a vampire.

The realization hit her so hard she wished she could sit down. Her legs suddenly seemed unsteady. "She lied to me, Bea, and all I wanted to do was ask her about it, and she said such horrible things. I had to go."

The tips of Beatrix's ears turned red, and she toed a clump of grass that had come loose from the ground. "About the... about the hourglass?"

"Yes." Calla shoved her hands into her pockets. It was freezing outside, and she'd forgotten a jacket. "About the goddamn hourglass counting down to who knows what." She looked at Beatrix but her eyes were on the ground. "You know what, don't you? You know what happens at the end?"

"I can't say."

Calla laughed. She'd heard the line before. She turned to go back into the motel.

"No, Calla. I can't say. It's not unsafe or something I don't want to say. I can't tell you. She couldn't even show you. She had to hide it."

Calla spun around, nausea rising in her stomach. "And let me break in to see it. No." She shook her head. It didn't make sense. She'd been so mad. "No. That's bullshit. She was furious."

"I do not think she believed you would break in so soon. It is... it is a delicate thing, the hourglass." Beatrix hugged her arms across her body, and looked like she would rather sink into the ground, but she kept talking. "Will you give her another chance?"

Calla held up a hand. She needed to get her thoughts in order before she could even think of giving Isolde a second chance. She breathed in the cold air and closed her eyes. When she opened them everything was the same. Beatrix in her stretched sweater, dead plants, a lonely highway, and Calla's heart beating too fast. "I need to leave."

The wind picked up, pulling at the loose strands of Beatrix's hair. "Don't go too far, just let me try something. Okay? The magic is dwindling. The time is running out. If you won't give Isolde another chance, will you give me one?"

"Okay," Calla said. What choice did she have? If she didn't, she knew she would spend her whole life wondering.

In one quick motion, Beatrix threw her arms around Calla's shoulders and pulled her into a tight embrace. "Be safe. Here." She pulled back, reached into the purse hanging at her side, and pulled out a stack of bills.

Calla almost declined, but she'd rather eat than have the moral high ground. She shoved the money into her pocket. "Beatrix, you be safe too. The thing you can't tell me..." But she didn't know what she wanted to ask. Possibilities swirled through her head like moths around a flame. Could she play a game of chicken with whatever magic had been done? Guess until Beatrix couldn't answer? There were too many options.

"If I don't—" Beatrix inhaled. "I wish you'd come back."

"I need space. I need to figure some things out." Her jaw hurt from clenching it. As Beatrix said a final goodbye and started to walk towards her car, Calla almost grabbed her, almost jumped in with her and went back.

But in the end she watched her drive away, watched until Beatrix's car was a speck in the road and her fingers were frozen. And then she went back inside to the drafty motel room and told Lisbet and her mother they'd get dinner and a nicer place to stay that night.

She didn't mention the hourglass. Didn't mention how viscerally she missed Isolde after only hours away. "I'll drive," she said, grabbing the keys off the table. "But I need to get the fuck out of here."

The day was clear, bright sunlight streaming through the bare branches of the trees on either side of the highway. They could have taken the interstate but Calla was in no rush. She rarely got out of New Dunwich and spent even less time in the country. She enjoyed the open fields, the occasional wild animal sighting and the rolling hills.

But by noon, Delphine and Lisbet were complaining of empty stomachs and Calla wasn't far behind them. They'd made their last few meals out of vending machines and her only source of protein had been a questionably edible Slim Jim.

They'd passed a couple gas stations, but none of them promised anything better than hot dogs off the roller. So they kept going, following signs for a town Calla had never heard of. She wanted something hot, specifically she wanted pancakes with a double side of sausage, but she'd settle for any meal served to her by someone else.

She grew more hopeful for a good meal the closer they got, empty stretches of highway giving way to farmhouses and then little subdivisions. She wondered what it would be like to live somewhere like this, only seeing other humans when she wanted to. She could get a job somewhere, buy a little house and learn to garden.

She doubted they were too worried about vampires in a place like this and even less worried about hunters. She could blend in. But it was all bullshit, Calla would miss the city, would miss late night pizza and walking everywhere. Her life, her new life, was just beginning. Small towns were good for plenty of people, but it wasn't where she wanted to set down roots.

Thinking of the future made her think of Isolde. Would she listen if Beatrix did whatever she was trying to do? And what could the secret Isolde held even be? Would it matter? Calla pulled her thoughts back. She wanted to talk to Lisbet about it but her mother was always there now, and as much as she loved her, as much as she told people her mother was her best friend, she did not want to discuss Isolde with her. Maybe they could leave her at the hotel that night, go on a walk and talk things out.

They came around a curve in the road and the town opened up, just a few streets with empty parking spots outside of a main stretch, but it was something. It definitely wasn't where Calla would spend her life, but it was adorable and maybe they could spend the night there.

"There!" Lisbet pointed to a restaurant with a red shingled roof and a giant, smiling, pancake painted on the side.

"Sold." Calla pulled into the gas station next door to The Pancake Palace. "I'll fill up and you guys can go get a table."

Her mother kissed the top of her head. "I've got to piss." She got out of the car and ran across the parking lot.

"Can we talk later? I need best friend advice?" Calla asked, getting out of the car and pulling her debit card out of her back pocket.

"Obviously yes. Do you have enough money to get your mom her own hotel room tonight? We can have a little sleepover."

"That sounds perfect." Calla swiped her card. "Will you get me a Coke Zero?"

"On it." Lisbet shut the car door and headed for the restaurant.

Calla leaned on the car and rested her head against the window, willing her thoughts away from Isolde. There was no real use to worrying until she heard back from Beatrix. Whatever she had to say could change everything or it could change nothing. And besides, she had breakfast food in her future. Everything would be better after a little maple syrup.

She turned and watched the numbers roll across the screen. She needed to get to a bank and deposit the money Beatrix had given her or she was going to overdraft soon. The pump clicked off, and she grabbed the nozzle and put it back.

She reached for the car handle, and someone grabbed her by the back of the head, smashing her face into the window. She felt her nose crunch. She rammed her head back and whoever was holding her grunted, their grasp loosening. Blood trickled from her nose into her mouth.

She twisted around and found Gus looking at her, a knot already swelling on his forehead. Relief washed over her. She could get away from Gus. She pulled herself from his grip and punched him. He stumbled back. Calla briefly considered thoroughly kicking his ass on her own, but instead she headed towards the Pancake Palace. Three was better than one.

She slipped between the pumps, and a body blocked her. "Fuck." She knew her. Erica Thomas, another hunter. Then another stepped out. She hadn't even noticed. Had they been following her? She glanced around, trying to find an escape route but there were half a dozen hunters in the gas station.

She tried to tell herself someone would notice but who would intervene? So she screamed, hoping her mother or Lisbet would hear. But it was a mistake. She was still for too long. They were upon her, fists colliding with her side, her head. She pushed one off just for another to grab her.

She tried to keep her hands apart when she noticed the rope, but they had her on the ground. She scrambled forward, the asphalt tearing at her skin. Someone kicked her, and she heard her rib crack. Pain flooded through her. Another kick.

Calla tried to scream again, but she wasn't sure if any sound came out. Her vision blurred. She thought she heard her mother but someone hoisted her up over their shoulder. She managed to kick them but the movement sent a wave of pain through her body.

Whoever was carrying her stopped and Gus's distorted face came into view. How had this happened? "Time to pay, bitch."

She spat a mouthful of blood in his face and was rewarded with being dropped onto the ground. A fresh pain shot through her elbow as she hit the concrete, and the edge of her vision went black. She was back in the air and she tried to stay focused. She needed to get away.

But the black kept growing and she no longer heard her mother.

When she woke up, the first thing she noticed, after the pain, was that she knew exactly where she was.

| Eighteen |

THE holding cells in the Council had been built for vampires. Though there were no windows on the walls the ceiling was made of thick, covered glass. At the moment Calla wished it was uncovered. She had no idea what time it was.

Every inch of her body hurt. There was no mirror, but she could feel the crusted blood on her face. She was going to murder Gus. Not even figuratively. She was going to snap his neck.

"Hey!" she yelled towards the door. She pushed herself up and looked around. She was in the same clothes she had been wearing at the gas station, but someone had taken her shoes off. There was an iron shackle around her ankle, connected by a thick chain to the concrete floor. She lifted her shirt and sucked in a breath. Several ribs were definitely broken, and there was a nasty purple bruise blooming across her chest.

Overall, nothing seemed life threatening. Her hunter's healing would take care of it all in a day or two. If she lived that long. Though she was full of murderous rage, she didn't know how she would actually get out of this.

The sound of a key in the lock got her attention, and she swiveled her body towards the door. Gus stepped inside carrying a tray of food. "I would recommend you not move."

"Fuck you." But she didn't move, except to brace her hands on the bed, ready to jump up if she needed to.

Gus sighed, put the tray of food down on the only table in the room, and glanced towards the door. Calla was sure there were more hunters out there, waiting to make sure she didn't enact her plans to murder him. He pulled a chair away from the wall and sat across from her. "There are ways we could move forward." He reached out, trying to brush a piece of her hair behind her ear, but it was too crusted with blood to move and pulled against her scalp. Memories of Isolde, bloody and dying in the backseat of a car, came flooding back.

Calla flinched away from him. "How could you? Why are you doing this to me?" Though she'd never seen eye to eye with Gus, if anyone had asked, she would have said she trusted him with her life. She'd trusted the whole Council with her life. And they'd tried to take it.

"You betrayed us, Calla." Gus was close enough that she could smell the whiskey on his breath underneath his cologne.

"The Council asked me to do it. I was following orders." There had to be a way out of this. There had to be a plan. But Calla couldn't see one.

His fist slammed into the wall behind her head. "Not true orders!" He stood up, looming over her, and for a moment she thought he would leave, but he bent down. "We could have been something, Calla. We could have ruled the Council."

She dug her fingers into the sheets of the bed to keep from reaching up and strangling him. Where was her mother? Lisbet? Did they know where she was? She looked into Gus's eyes, and the whispers of a plan appeared to her. She let go of the sheets, tried to relax her face, let her lip quiver. "I only wanted to protect my mother. I was so scared, Gus. Please, don't do this to me."

He sat back in his chair. "I saw you at the gala. Don't lie to me, Calla."

"I'm *not*. I was doing what I was told, but I should have listened to you. I should have stood with you from the beginning, done what I knew my mother would have preferred. She would rather rot than have me live with a vampire." She scooted closer to the edge of the bed.

"You disappointed me."

"I know." She dropped her gaze to the floor. "I'm sorry."

"I'll bring a basin so you can wash up. And eat." He pointed to the plate of food. "Tomorrow you will tell us all your secrets, by choice or by force." He left and Calla heard the lock click behind him.

The food was simple, a handful of crackers and a revolting looking stew. It was also cold. But Calla ate it anyway. She'd need strength. She'd also need to come up with something to tell Gus and his crew, something that they would believe.

She had made her way back to the bed when the door opened, and a woman Calla vaguely recognized brought in the promised basin of water. She didn't make eye contact, or even glance in Calla's direction. She left the basin on the floor and when she left the lock clicked behind her.

Calla washed without a mirror. The rag came away red, staining the water and she wished she could think of anything but Isolde. The vampire had told her that the estate was the safest place for her, but Calla never listened and now she might die for it. Her best chance of survival was making Gus believe she might care for him, but she'd spent her whole life trying to convince him she didn't.

For the first time in her life, Calla felt truly hopeless. She laid down, the hard floor cold on her back, and stared at the ceiling. Were the stars or the sun above her? She hoped the stars were out, that Isolde was awake, maybe thinking of Calla too.

In the empty cell, all of Isolde's crimes didn't seem as large as they had when they were screaming at each other. The vampire had spent hundreds of years keeping herself alive. Like Calla her whole world had flipped, leaving her flailing. And Calla had let her believe she might catch her, that even if they fell, it would be in each other's arms. And then she'd run.

All she had ever done was run. In each of her brief relationships, she'd run when things got hard. She spent her whole life fighting, so she'd never bothered in her personal relationships. She'd kept them short, bed warmers who spent the night and left. It was easier that way. She'd say she would change, let Lisbet set her up, and then she wouldn't call.

She banged her head against the floor. Why was she worried about this now? She was trapped, probably about to be tortured, and all she could think of was the vampire who had trapped her first.

Now she might never learn the secret of the hourglass, whatever horrible thing had Isolde terrified. There was so much more about Isolde she wanted to learn, and some part of her had believed there would be more time. She had stormed out, but the possibility of going back had been there, rolling around in the back of her mind.

How would Gus do it? Hanging? Poison? Bleeding her out? Unexpectedly, she heard a cranking noise and the covering for the roof opened revealing inky darkness. There were no stars to be seen; she was in the middle of the city, surrounded by millions of people, and not one of them would save her.

Did they know who had blown up the gala? Was this the desperate flailing of a man in trouble or the beginnings of a dictator? Calla suspected the first, could not see Gus leading a larger army than the hunters he had known all his life.

Closing her eyes, Calla thought of Isolde, the soft silk of her skin, the gold of her hair. Isolde was strange, both gentle and commanding, harsh and vivacious. She could have gotten to know her, but despite her best efforts Calla had been born a hunter and now, it seemed, that was how she would die.

The floor was cold but she couldn't be bothered to move. Her bed would be no better.

| Nineteen |

ONCE again, Calla woke in the most unpleasant way, without enough time to appreciate the sunlight streaming in from above her. This time it was not just Gus, there were a dozen hunters and Council members in her room. She'd known most of them since she was small, though a few had seemingly flown in for this. The expressions staring at her changed with each face, disgust, pity, hate.

"Get up," an older woman named Beth said, but she didn't give Calla time before dragging her up by her hair.

Calla's hands shot up, gripping Beth's wrists before she remembered where she was. She could smash Beth to the floor, watch her head bounce off the concrete and her face go slack, but there was no way she could get through everyone in the building.

The others moved forward as Beth stiffened, but Calla dropped her hands before anyone reacted. Still, she knew she would regret it. She watched the pity evaporate from their faces, anger turn into rage.

Shackles were placed around her wrists while another Council member removed the chain to the floor. She watched as he put the key in his pocket. If she picked the lock, would she be able to get to the ceiling and break the glass? Probably not without something hard, and there was nothing nearby.

Beth pushed her shoulder, and she stumbled forward, pressing her lips together to keep from saying anything. The hunters and Council members closed in around her. At least they knew she was dangerous.

She thought of fighting her way free. Maybe if she got closer to the door. This was her best chance, free of the cell, her legs free. But still she followed, outnumbered and bound.

Her heart ached with each step, a prisoner in the place she had once loved. She wanted it back, wanted to force Gus to his knees, remove him from the Council headquarters. She was a hunter, she was the best hunter. How dare he treat her this way? She cut her eyes at him and found him staring back.

"Look at all you gave up," he said.

I gave up nothing. You have stolen something you could never understand. A castle you will never keep. "Perhaps I will earn it back." Defiance danced inside her, and it took all her willpower not to fight back. But she needed to save her strength, if she could not manage to sweet talk Gus she would have to force her way out—or rot in a cell. If they weren't walking her to a torture chamber right now.

"Here." Gus grabbed her by her upper arm and shoved her through double doors.

"Are you serious?" Calla hissed, looking around at the Council's chambers. "Am I on trial?" Her best intentions evaporated like mist in the sun. She would not be able to sweet talk him. This was a mockery of the trials they once held, and she could already guess how it would end. She had been stupid to hope otherwise.

Everyone streamed in, several of them taking seats at the table in front of her. Was this all their numbers? She looked around. He had less than twenty. Enough to cause a stir, enough to hold her for now. But not enough. How had they ousted the rest of the Council? If this was all of his allies, or at least all he kept in the building, then escape did not seem so unlikely.

She leaned back, staring up at the table, at Gus who sat in the middle. How could they rally behind him? What had he ever done to earn his place in the top ranks of the Council? What had he ever done for the hunters? She had hated vampires too, but never enough to betray her own people. Gus might accuse her of it, but he was the real traitor.

The room settled and Gus stared down at her. "Calla Chase you are accused of cavorting with vampires, of betraying the Council and forsaking your vows. What do you say to these charges?"

Calla let out a hollow laugh that echoed through the room. "I say I do not recognize your authority to question me. I say you are a lesser Council member who has not earned the seat you sit in."

"Disappointing." He smirked. "But luckily the Council—"

"Gus Cadieux you do not speak for the Council!" Calla pulled against her restraints. There was movement behind her, and she turned her head in time to see a flash of flesh as a fist slammed against her face. She spit out blood. "Fuck you, Everett. Your family hasn't had the hunter power in generations. You were only here as a courtesy. Untie me and hit me again."

Everett leaned down. He'd always been close to Gus and never worth anything. She'd heard whispers of his family losing Council status. No wonder he'd jumped at this opportunity. "You forget your place."

Calla grinned. "I look around and all I see is jealousy. Weak hunters. Council members who would never rise. The bottom rings of this organization. Do what you must to me, but I will *never* answer to you. Mother Nature gave me my power. You have no authority to take it."

"Step back, Everett," Gus said, gavel in hand. "Calla, stop grandstanding." He stood up, walking around the table and sat on the other side, only feet from her. "What are the vampires' plans?"

She couldn't help but laugh. "She *really* wanted me to be her girlfriend."

A muscle in his jaw twitched. He looked like hell. His hair was a greasy mess, there were bags under his eyes. She hoped he couldn't sleep at night. "Calla, don't make us hurt you."

"You asked. I answered."

"I do not mean Isolde, what are the plans of all the vampires?"

"How the fuck am I supposed to know?" She sat up straighter. "I met a grand total of one other vampire while I was there. But I don't think they have any major plans. You're the one blowing shit up, Gus. They're just trying to live."

"Wow." He clicked his tongue and pushed himself off the table. He leaned forward, lowering his voice, his next question was just for her. "Did you fuck her, Calla?"

"Yes. I'd rather fuck a vampire than you." She stared into his eyes, expecting hate but it was hurt that flashed through them. Good. "And it was great, Gus. Best sex I've ever had." He slapped her. The impact left her face stinging, and she laughed again. "Would you let me go, Gus? If I crawled into bed? That's why I'm here isn't it? This is the only way you could have me."

"You have no idea what you're talking about."

She ran her tongue over her split lip, tasting blood. "Don't I? Should I have begged? I considered it." She batted her lashes. "Oh Gus, I'd do anything for my freedom. Please, let me suck your big cock."

His cheeks turned red.

"Gus." Everett stepped forward. "I do not think we are going to get answers from her. Not yet." He leaned closer, whispering something Calla couldn't hear.

Was this all? Had they dragged her here for this? But no, it would not be that easy. This was the show, the thing they could point to and say they tried. This was how they soothed their guilty conscience. There would be more, this was only the beginning.

"Fine," Gus said, running his hand through his dark hair. "Take her back to her cell. Perhaps she will answer when she is hungry."

Calla's stomach swooped. They were going to starve her. She needed to figure out a way to get the fuck out of this place and fast, before she was too weak to do it.

But she was rechained, bound and dragged by too many to fight. She had been afraid before, but her heart pounded as they left her room. She didn't fight when they shoved her into the room, nor when they shackled her to the floor. She was outnumbered, and no plan came to her, no way out of this.

"Enjoy the view," Beth said and then Calla was alone.

| Twenty |

THREE days had passed since Calla had seen another person. Above her bed, the sun was giving way to night, just as it had been the day before when she'd eaten the last of the food she'd hidden away. Three crackers.

Would they really let her starve? Except she knew the answer. No one was going to let her starve, but they were going to let her come close. And then what? She had no answers for them. What did the vampires want? The only answer she had—peace—wasn't going to satisfy anyone in that room.

And now she was too weak to fight. Too weak to plan any kind of escape. Her stomach grumbled and ached, and she shifted on the bed, but there was no relief to be found. How long could a person last without food? She'd read about it once, but she couldn't remember.

She'd watched the blue of the sky fade to pink then purple before turning black. It was all there was to do. Something moved above her. Bats had been flying over the skylight all night, just as they had the night before. They must live nearby.

She settled into the bed to watch them fully and found Biyu staring back at her. Her heart beat faster. Was she hallucinating? But Biyu knocked on the glass. Calla stood on her bed, straining her neck to stare up. She wanted to scream, to fall to her knees and weep. She was afraid anything she did would alert whoever was in the building. So she just stood, trembling and hungry on her bed.

Biyu mouthed something, but a commotion in the hallway tore Calla's attention away until Biyu banged on the sunroof, cracking the glass. The vampire pointed frantically towards the wall.

"What?" Calla mouthed back.

Move!" Biyu's voice barely reached her, but Calla did as she was told, scrambling back and pressing her body against the cinderblock wall.

Someone screamed, and Calla looked back up, but Biyu was no longer above her, just the open expanse of the night sky. Her heart pounded in her chest, and she dug her fingers into the divots between the cinder blocks that made up the wall.

For the second time in her life the room exploded around Calla, and she dropped to the ground, covering her head. Smoke filled the room burning her eyes. When the ground stopped trembling, she waved her hands in front of her face, trying to see.

"Calla!" Isolde's voice was desperate.

Calla lurched forward, a sob escaping her lips and ran, but her shackles were shorter than the distance to Isolde and she tripped. Before she could hit the ground she was in Isolde's arms. Plaster dust covered the vampire's face, streaked with blood that dripped down her chin and onto her clothes.

"Isolde." Calla reached out and brushed the dust off her cheek. The smell of blood was thick in the air but Calla couldn't see any wounds on Isolde. She swallowed.

"We've got to go," Isolde said.

"I can't." Calla swallowed, rattling the shackle on her ankle.

"Hurry the fuck up," Biyu said, appearing in the doorway. Her gaze caught on the shackles. "Shit." She rushed forward. "Come on, put her down and help me." She wrapped her delicate fingers around the metal. Isolde put Calla gently on the floor, and joined Biyu, smearing the chains with blood.

Together the two vampires pulled. The chains groaned. They pulled again. The ground cracked but didn't give. Calla yanked her leg, and the chain pulled free, though it dangled heavy from her ankle.

"No matter," Isolde grabbed Calla and cradled her in her arms. "Hold on."

Calla did as she was told, wrapping her arms around Isolde's neck. Blood was sticky between them. There was so much she wanted to say, so many words hiding behind her lips, but now was not the time.

Outside her cell she expected chaos, but it was eerily silent. Calla nearly buried her face in the crook of Isolde's neck, but she made herself witness the scene they moved through, the wide splatters of blood, the twisted bodies. She knew these people, their mouths agape, their eyes wide. She had laughed with them once.

Now they were dead, and Calla didn't know if she should blame them or herself. Together they had brought Isolde down upon the Council. All of them were dead, the vampire's wrath clear in the way they were not just murdered but mangled. Calla had wanted her freedom but Isolde had wanted revenge and she had gotten it.

Gus was nowhere to be seen. Of course. He would not make up the night watch. These were the weakest hunters, the ones desperate to prove something. None of them were a match for a seven hundred-year-old vampire. Had the others fled? She hoped they had, and that they would not return. But though she felt mercy, she could summon no sympathy for the dead.

As they emerged from the Council building, Calla gulped down the first fresh air she'd had in a week. Sirens blared in the distance. Someone cursed and then she was out of Isolde's arms, wrapped in the soft leather of her car and the vampire slid in beside her.

"Glad you're alive," Beatrix said from the front seat as Biyu slammed the door shut, and the car lurched to a start.

Was this real? Calla's head swam with the last ten minutes. But Isolde was there. Isolde had saved her. She turned, the shackles still heavy on her ankles. Tear tracks ran through the plaster dust on Isolde's face, and all the anger that had twisted her features in the Council building was gone. "Why are you crying?"

"I'm so sorry." Isolde gripped Calla's legs. "All you wanted was the truth. I should not have screamed at you. I should not have driven you away."

Though she knew she should be angry, Calla couldn't muster anything other than relief. She had sworn her life to the Council, and they had sold her to a vampire and then starved her for it. The Council may be split but Calla wanted nothing to do with either side. "I forgive you," she said. "I thought I would die in there. And you saved me. So we're even."

"Oh, how I wish we were." Isolde's voice wavered, and she gripped Calla's knee.

Calla took one of Isolde's hands and pulled it to her lap. Tears formed in her eyes, and she blinked, letting them fall. "Are you going to get in trouble for that?" She glanced up at Isolde. The vampire sniffled, wiping at her tears and smearing more plaster across her face. God, she should be mad. She should be terrified at the extent of what Isolde was willing to do, but she wasn't.

Even though she was covered in blood, all Calla could think about was kissing her. She wanted to feel Isolde wrapped around her, her breath cool on Calla's thighs, her teeth sharp. Calla wanted to go back to her house, and she never wanted to leave. She was tired of trying to convince herself she didn't feel the way she did. Tired of pretending she didn't want Isolde. Even covered in blood, the proof of her sins still on her skin, Calla wanted Isolde more desperately than she had ever wanted anything.

"Despite what recent events may have led you to believe, I am good at covering my tracks. Biyu took care of the security cameras on the block, and I have enough money and connections. Don't worry about consequences." Isolde scooted closer. "Calla, are you okay?"

"I'm starving. I haven't eaten in days." The adrenaline of her escape was draining from her body. She was starving, in a very real way.

"Bastards," Biyu muttered from the front seat. There was a crinkling of paper as she continued to curse the Council, and then she pulled something from her purse. "Sorry, this is all I have." She tossed a pack of cheese crackers into the backseat.

Calla pulled them open, inhaling their scent. She didn't even care why Biyu had them with her. Baked cheese products had never smelled so good. She shoved a handful into her mouth.

Isolde didn't take her eyes off of Calla, and under normal circumstances she might have felt embarrassed as she upturned the package and dumped the rest into her mouth, but Isolde had rescued her.

She had come for Calla. She had saved her. Calla wiped her mouth. "Have you seen my mother?"

"No, but she's safe. So is Lisbet." Isolde let go of Calla and pulled out her phone. "I'll tell Molly to get your room ready and—"

"No." Calla moved closer. "No. I don't want to be alone. Stay with me."

Someone honked, and the car swerved. Isolde's knees banged against Calla's legs. Her eyes narrowed, and her lips kept moving as though she wanted to say something but no words came out.

"It's okay, love. They aren't going to get you again." Biyu twisted in her seat. "I swear it. I've had enough. We're—"

"Not now," Isolde said, without taking her eyes off of Calla. "We'll tell her everything when we get home." She took Calla's face in her hands. "I'll tell you everything. Everything."

The truth. Isolde was promising her the truth. She had a million questions, but they flew like birds, too fast, too high for her to grasp them. As long as she knew the truth they could find a way forward. "I can't believe I let them take me."

"No. Don't think like that. There's no good there," Isolde said.

All the worst moments in Calla's life seemed to be followed by riding in the backseat of this car, but looking into Isolde's timeless face, Calla felt safe. She unbuckled her seatbelt and laid down, resting her head in Isolde's lap. She stroked Calla's hair as the gentle noises of the highway lulled her to sleep.

| Twenty One |

WHEN Calla awoke, the smell of smoke and spice surrounded her. This had to be the best day of her life, the day she was back in the place she wished she had never left. Every moment since she had stormed out of Isolde's had been a nightmare she could not wake from. She snuggled deeper into Isolde's fur covered bed, and dreaded opening her eyes because for just that moment she was happy, safe, untroubled.

Calla had been hurt before. She'd had the shit kicked out of her by vampires. She'd hidden in places, cold and hungry. But usually Calla did the rescuing. Usually, she was the one carrying someone to safety. But for the last few months Calla had been falling, hating herself, unsure of who she was. She had been falling, but at the bottom she'd found someone waiting to catch her.

The bed shifted, and she opened her eyes just enough to see Isolde slip under the sheets with her. She pulled Calla close, tangling their bare legs together. She pressed her lips to Calla's forehead. "It will be dawn soon."

"I wish you could stay," Calla murmured into Isolde's neck, then she moved lower, kissing her collarbone, the soft skin between her breasts, breathing in the scent of her.

"So do I. But I never can, Calla. And..." Isolde's body tensed, and Calla opened her eyes.

The room was still dark, the only light illuminating Isolde's face was from a single flickering candle. Calla was surprised to find tears streaking her cheeks. She brushed one away with her thumb. "Don't cry. I'm sorry for all the things I said." All her anger at Isolde seemed so far away now, something someone else had felt. Now, being here, back in this bed, was the most wonderful thing she could imagine. She'd spent her whole life angry. She was ready to try something new. "I'll cooperate with the police. We can have him arrested, and you won't have to worry about him anymore. I know all the places he could hide. I'll side with the vampires. I don't care about any of that anymore, Isolde."

Her crying deepened, whimpers turning into sobs. "Oh, Calla. They broke the curse, but..."

"Tell me, baby. Whatever it is."

Isolde sat up, hugging a pillow to her chest. She no longer looked like the frightening woman she had when they had met. Calla could see the scared girl she had been when she was turned, young and innocent, just trying to protect herself. All those centuries walking the world, hidden in shadows, becoming someone else, someone who she wasn't at her core.

Calla sat up, resisting the urge to say something. They had today, at least. She was sure Gus was off somewhere licking his wounds. For today, she felt safe. There was time to let Isolde finally say the words she had not been allowed to speak. She reached out, pulling one of Isolde's hands into her lap. She ran her fingers over her skin, feeling the veins and joints beneath.

"My staff are the descendants of witches," Isolde said.

Calla just nodded. Whatever she had expected, it wasn't that.

"But not the witches who cursed me. They are the descendants of the witches who created vampires, and I have spent centuries finding them. Protecting them. My blood is from the original line, the first vampire they created. After they made him, they made others, but his was the original line and his blood was the strongest. They gave less power to those who came after, less strength, less..." Isolde shrugged. "As I told you before, I do not know, truly. I have only heard the stories."

Calla waited, still clutching Isolde's hand in her own. This part she knew. Now she waited to hear how it was all connected.

"A woman found me not long after I was made. She came to the house I was sheltering in one night. She was thin and trembled with the cold, but her voice was strong. She told me she had something that had belonged to my maker, and now it belonged to me. It was the hourglass, hidden beneath her cloak. She gave it to me, and then she was gone, disappeared into the wind and the snow."

Calla scooted closer. "What did it mean? How did she find you?"

Isolde's lips twitched, the closest thing to a smile that Calla had seen all night. "I had no idea, but I could feel the magic on it in a way I never had before. I could feel the life in it, tied to my own. It took me a long time to track down the truth of that hourglass. That is part of why I have such an extensive library. And with each passing year the blood fell, slowly at first and then faster. I put it off as much as I could. I brought it to witches and begged for help, did favors, threatened them, but now the magic of the witches is but a trickle, and I can not stop the inevitable."

"But what does it mean?" Calla brought Isolde's hand to her mouth and kissed her fingers. It was all she could do, touch a part of her, remind Isolde that she was not alone.

"I should have never touched it. I think if I hadn't ever gotten close to it, then it wouldn't have imprinted on me. The spell was meant for him, a curse on the original vampire, and the witches who created him. Not me. But the woman who brought it must have known that. She wanted to punish me for his sins."

"What does it mean, Isolde?" Calla repeated her question, but she was afraid of the answer. Afraid of the pressure that rose in her chest, the way her stomach knotted. "Do you die when all the blood falls?"

Isolde nodded. "And I am not sure, but I think we all die. I think they can feel it just as I can. I should never have brought them here."

"What is the curse?"

"I brought soup." Isolde stood, pulling her hand from Calla, and inclined her head towards a covered dish on the dresser. The look in her eyes was pleading.

Calla understood. She needed space to say it, a revelation she had never spoken aloud before. She walked to the dresser. "Who broke the..." Spell? Magic? What had held Isolde's tongue? She took the lid from the pot and the aroma of rosemary and sage made her mouth water. It was a thin soup with pieces of carrots and chicken bobbing in broth, the perfect meal, cozy and simple.

"Beatrix. She still practices simple magics, healing tonics, incantations to goddesses. There is still magic in the world, but it has become harder to harness."

Calla nodded, ladling soup into one of the bowls sitting beside the tray. She took a tentative sip, and it warmed her as it slid down her throat. So much better than the cheese crackers Biyu had given her.

Outside the window she could see the first signs of dawn, the orange hue between the trees at the property's edge. Soon Isolde would need to go to sleep, and Calla knew fear would creep in. She sat on the windowsill, curling her feet underneath her. "Is this the first time you've talked about the curse."

"No. I told Biyu and Beatrix. But telling you is different. Still, nothing to be done but doing it." Isolde took a deep breath, her chest rising and falling, her eyes briefly fluttering shut. "I must find love, real human love, before the last drop of blood falls. Then I must turn that human."

The bowl fell from Calla's fingers, soup seeping into the rug. Her lungs constricted. She didn't know what terrified her more; falling in love with a vampire or becoming one. She stood, unable to take her eyes off Isolde. Beautiful, frightening, incredible Isolde.

Isolde came around the bed and stood in front of Calla, trembling. "Please understand, I am not asking that of you, sweet darling mortal. I never would."

"How exactly does it work? Being made into a vampire?" Isolde had mentioned it before, but that was just to assure her she wasn't changing. Calla needed to know all of it.

Isolde kissed Calla, brief and soft. Her lips were barely there before they were gone, but the taste of her lingered. "We would share blood. I would drink yours, you would drink mine. We would gorge ourselves on each other until our life forces were mixed. Then you must die. The most common way is for me to drain you completely, but any way of dying will work as long as it is at my hands. A vampire is never a mistake. Making another vampire is a choice. Then you must come back, and the choice will no longer be mine, it will be yours. You would need to drink from a human, or the next time you slept you would not wake."

Calla nodded. "The books were right. I always thought it would be more complicated." She waited, not wanting to say the next part, the thing that had hung over her the entire time she had been trapped in the Council building. Isolde didn't say anything either, even while her eyes searched Calla—though what they looked for, Calla didn't know.

She brushed her thumb over Isolde's cheek, the cool, smooth skin. She wanted her more desperately than she had ever wanted anything before. Her want was deeper than the space between her legs, than heavy breathing and nights spent together. She wanted everything, she wanted to know her, all the hidden parts. She wanted to hear all her stories and help create her new adventures. She wanted her safe, not dead, cursed by a long gone witch. "I love you, Isolde. I do."

The estate fell silent, or maybe Calla only wanted it to. She started to move forward, to pull Isolde towards her, to kiss her properly for the first time in too long, but the vampire fell to her knees with a horrible wail.

Calla dropped as well. "Isolde?"

"You must run. You must leave here. I can not do the rest, Calla. I can not. And if they find out, even Beatrix or Molly, they will demand I turn you." She looked up, tears dripping from her eyelashes and running down her cheeks. "And I want to. More than you can know. I want you with me. I am so tired of being alone."

Calla wrapped Isolde in her arms. "They weren't forcing you before. They won't now."

Isolde laughed coldly. "Because love can not be forced, but look how they tried. Dressing you up, endearing me to you. None of us could voice the curse, but we all knew it. They could feel it in their heartbeats, the way each drop took a little of their life as it fell. You can not blame them, Calla. They have not had as many lifetimes as I have. They are not ready to die."

"It will be all the descendants of witches."

"No." Isolde shook her head. "No, and I can not explain it exactly. It follows the blood of those who made vampires, it follows those who still wish to practice, who seek us out."

Calla's arms dropped, leaving them both sitting on the soup stained carpet, the scent of it permeating the room. "And if I turn, it will save them?" The words scratched at her throat, the knowledge tearing her up from the inside. She had protected others her whole life, fought for their safety. But this was different. This was not dying for them, this was something else. Living without. Giving up the things she loved. Giving up the sun.

"No. Not if *you* turn. If I turn you. And I will not." Isolde lurched forward, grabbing Calla too roughly, pinching her flesh beneath her nails. "I love you too, Calla. When you came here, I hoped I would not. I prayed there would be no love between us and this whole thing would be over. But I do love you, Calla, and I will not turn you. I will not have you live as I have lived."

"Isolde." Calla brushed the hair away from her face. She had never seen her look so wild and distraught. She kissed her, each eyelid, her cheeks, and then her lips. She kissed her slowly, pressing her tongue into Isolde's mouth, tasting her. Calla kissed her until she felt her relax in her arms, the tension in her body giving way. "Isolde, I love you."

Calla traced Isolde's jaw with her fingers, ran her nails down her neck, over her collarbone, across the peaked ridges of her nipples, nearly exposed under her silk nightgown. Part of Calla wanted to lay her down, to undress her and fuck her until they had both forgotten their problems, but she had to do this before she lost her nerve.

She brought her fingers back to Isolde's face and placed them under her chin, turning her face up to look at her. "I do not want to be a vampire, Isolde, but I also have spent my life protecting people. I know your life has been hard, but that would not be what you are giving me. I wouldn't be alone, I would have you. And you would have me. Forever." But the words were heavy, coating her tongue. She loved Isolde, but she did not know her well. Days would turn to months, to years, to centuries. How long would love last? How long until she resented her for it?

The soup was still spilled, glistening on the floor, and she thought of the cook who had made it, of Molly who must have carried it upstairs. She thought of the way they would die. And if Calla hated being a vampire, she could walk into the sun. She did not want it, but she could not bear for them to die. And there was a chance, a huge chance, that their love would last. They could be happy. They could spend centuries loving each other, exploring the world. Calla could see all the things she had been too busy to see before. And Isolde would live.

Whatever the future held, she wanted a chance at it. She wanted to find out. Her time with Isolde had been short and fraught with turmoil. She wanted a chance to love her properly, to know her without duress. She wanted to coax out the soft woman underneath and make love to her under the stars. And there was only one way to do that.

"You must turn me."

Isolde's body shook, but her eyes were bright and locked on Calla. She nodded, almost imperceptibly. "I am so tired." She glanced at the window, where the day was making itself known in pinks and reds.

Calla kissed her forehead. "We will talk about it later. We'll have forever."

| Twenty Two |

THE sun shone so brightly it seemed to mock Calla.

Goodbye. Farewell. So long.

Calla went to the kitchen. The cook was wiping down counters, gently humming. She'd untied her apron from around her neck and it hung from her waist. The descendant of a witch. Of course Isolde had witches working for her. She thought of Beatrix and pride swelled inside her chest. She'd broken the curse. As far as Calla was concerned, Beatrix wasn't the descendant of a witch, she was a witch and the most badass one Calla knew.

"What's your name?" Calla asked the cook.

She turned towards Calla. "Eleanor." She smiled. "Did you like your soup?"

"I'm afraid I spilled it, but the little bit I had was absolutely delicious." Calla rummaged through the fridge, pulling out the ingredients for a sandwich. "How long have you worked here? She's a vampire, why does she even need a cook?"

"She has a staff and they all eat. Here." Eleanor took the ingredients from Calla. "Are you okay? We heard what happened."

"Not really but I will be... eventually." Because she would have forever. The kitchen seemed to grow small. Calla gripped the counter for support. As soon as Eleanor was done, she grabbed the sandwich. "Sorry,

I just need air." She pushed open the door to the patio, but it was too enclosed. Holding the plate tightly, Calla kept walking.

Something moved in the woods at the edge of the property, and Calla came to a stop. Though it was only a squirrel bounding through the branches, her heart pounded. For a moment, the thought of becoming a vampire had driven the danger she was in out of her mind. She sunk down into the grass, still wet and cold with morning dew, and took a bite of her sandwich.

There was nothing Calla could do about the danger of the former Council members, but she could protect this house and everyone in it. And in the process she would protect herself, become stronger. When Gus struck again, she would have a surprise for him in the form of fangs.

Could she really do it? Calla had spent her whole life fighting vampires, and part of her still believed in the worthiness of that cause. She had seen the damage done by vampires. But humans murdered each other too, at higher rates and in more terrible ways. The more time she spent with them the more it seemed vampires were only extensions of the humans they had once been—stronger, sturdier, lonelier as the centuries passed, but still, at their core, who they were.

She could see it in Isolde. She still believed in so many things from the days she had been breathing, the proper way to do things, to dress and act and be. But she had traded her virtue for safety, and now Calla would do the same.

Fat clouds dotted the sky, and she laid back, letting the dew soak through her clothes. Soon the cold would no longer bother her. She imagined what it would be like to be a vampire, to drink blood. When disgust coiled its fingers around her stomach, she thought of Molly and

Beatrix. She thought of Isolde, mostly of Isolde. Whatever she felt about being a vampire it did not come close to how she felt about losing her.

She took a bite and sighed. *Isolde.* She should have seen this coming from the first time Isolde knocked her to the floor and she didn't stake her for it. She was the most frustrating woman Calla had ever met, full of contradictions created by too many lifetimes' worth of experiences.

Would Calla be the same one day? Would she hold on to antiquated things and cover her humanity in a hard shell? She thought of her mother—who she needed to check in with—not of what she would say, that was easy enough to guess, but how it would feel to watch her grow old while Calla did not age. How Lisbet's hair would gray, and her shoulders would sink, and eventually she would leave the world and Calla behind.

But, Calla was not stupid, eventually death would come for her too, even vampirism could not stop the reaper forever. The thought calmed her rapidly rising pulse. Her life had been in freefall since the vampires had come into the public eye, this was just another detour.

She finished the last of her sandwich and stood up, brushing grass off her clothes and went inside. She closed her eyes, and maybe it was magic or just her imagination, but she could feel the hourglass, the gentle pulse of it. And maybe it wasn't magic at all, maybe it was love, the love it had been waiting centuries for, the love it had almost given up on.

A thread pulled her, and she followed it through the labyrinth of the estate until she came to the library, bathed in sunlight. A woman she had seen working in the house was curled up, asleep in a chair with a book on her lap. Calla did her best to walk quietly, trying not to disturb her but committing her face to memory. A reason for her sacrifice.

199

Though full of books, the library was seemingly devoid of magically cursed hourglasses, but she still followed the thread that was pulling her until she came to a shadowed alcove with a single bookshelf tucked between two overstuffed chairs. She frowned, looking at the space. Maybe she had made up the whole feeling.

"I can't believe she told you," Beatrix said and Calla jumped, letting out a shrill shriek that made Beatrix laugh. "Sorry."

"Of course she told me," Calla said, turning around to face her.

"I knew she'd tell you about the curse, but I didn't think she'd tell you where it was." Beatrix sat in one of the chairs.

Calla raised an eyebrow. "She didn't. I just... well, is it invisible?"

Beatrix laughed and ran her finger under one of the emptier shelves. The wood creaked, and the bookshelf moved a fraction. "Go ahead. I'd want to see it too." Calla started to walk but Beatrix reached out, grabbing her arm. "Whatever you decide is okay with me. I won't blame you, either way."

Words escaped her and her tongue was too heavy to move, so she just brushed her hand over Beatrix's shoulder before pulling the bookshelf open. Inside just enough light shone to illuminate a pull-cord dangling from the ceiling. Calla pulled it and then descended the stairs in front of her.

She waited for something to feel wrong, after all she was walking down a hidden staircase after a cursed object, but fear and trepidation never came. As she went deeper into the earth, the air grew cooler. The staircase ended in a room lit by wall sconces. The space was simple, packed earth, a wooden table and open shelves on stone walls.

Each shelf was full of jars of little simples, crushed flowers, dried herbs and other things Calla could not identify. The last of the magics of the world, the gifts from mother earth that time could never deplete.

And in the middle of it all was the hourglass. The bottom was full of blood and above a single drop remained, suspended in air and glistening in the light. A beautiful, sanguine curse. She'd seen cursed objects before, the Council had a room full of them, but most were weapons, swords with twisted blades, hammers too heavy to lift. She'd never seen such cruel magic so wonderfully wrought.

Wrapping her hands around the bulbous glass, she held it up to the light. The whole thing vibrated with magic at her touch. Though the Council rarely spoke about it, Calla had known her whole life that there was magic in her veins, some vestige of power that witches had imbued the hunters with. She felt it when she struck, she felt it when she killed. Power, much larger than anything she could do on her own.

She sat the hourglass down just to resist the urge to smash the whole thing, though she doubted it would break, and then sat on the floor looking up at it. The first vampire. Calla had never given much thought to if vampires had different bloodlines. She knew they could have unique powers, some were better at manipulation, some were faster, almost too fast to see when they moved. She'd seen vampires that could levitate though they called it flying.

"Fuck you," she whispered to the hourglass and Beatrix squeezed her hand. "I don't want to be a vampire." She didn't understand it. Whoever made this must have hated vampires, why make another? She leaned back, staring up at the stone above her. She loved Isolde. She hadn't meant to, would never have believed she would love a vampire, part of her almost wished she didn't, but she did. That was the only good she could see. If she had to live all those years at least she wouldn't be alone.

One good thing in a sea of shit. She still had Gus to deal with and once she got turned, she was sure she'd be stuck front and center as the spokeswoman for vampire human relationships. There was a whole mess waiting for her, but first she had to get through this.

"There you are."

Calla hadn't even realized she had fallen asleep, but Biyu was standing over her, one hand on her hip, a slight smile parting her lips. She remembered asking Beatrix to give her some time alone, and then just staring, wishing, crying. "What time is it?"

"Not so late, but you have Isolde worried." Biyu pulled at her trousers and sat down beside Calla. "This is a terrible place to sleep for a human. Your back must hurt."

Calla sat up and stretched. Her back did hurt. "Does your back never hurt? Can I add that to the pros list?"

"Only in the most dire of circumstances and only temporarily, little human. So you will do it? Isolde explained it all to me. I'm sorry I upset you so badly you went and got yourself kidnapped. I can assure you that was not my intention."

"I know that." Calla sighed. "And maybe I could have listened before I started yelling. But this is all a lot for me. And not just this..." She gestured towards the hourglass. "But being around vampires without fighting. My world is upside down." She wasn't sure why she was spilling her heart to Biyu, but she wasn't sure why she was doing much lately.

"I understand." Biyu picked up the hourglass and frowned before setting it down. "I can't believe Isolde served in the Directorate, led so many of our campaigns and never told us she carried a ticking bomb. This explains many of her recent actions." Biyu nudged Calla, then stood and offered her hand to pull her up. "She is good though, Calla. I have loved her like a sister for many centuries, and she has been a loyal and steadfast friend, if a little... annoying at times."

Calla let herself be pulled to her feet. "Maybe we can be friends too, me and you. I'll need them. I'm sure Lisbet will hate me once she finds out what I plan to do."

Before Biyu could answer, footsteps sounded down the stairs, moving quickly until Isolde was in front of her. Calla wasn't sure what she expected, but it wasn't the scowl that appeared on the vampire's face. "What are you doing down here? I didn't know where you were."

Biyu slipped up the stairs while Calla stepped closer to Isolde. "I was not aware I had to inform you of all my comings and goings."

"When someone wants to kill you, you do! You were just kidnapped, and I had to rescue you and I don't want to do it again." Her gaze flickered to the hourglass. "Oh, Calla." Isolde scrubbed her hand over face. "You are my biggest frustration."

"Because I'm down here? That's your biggest problem?" Calla threw her arm out, knocking over the hourglass. It started to fall and then righted itself.

"Because I cannot get you out of my head. Because even when I sleep I dream of you. Because I wake in a panic if you are not next to me. You, a fragile human. A hunter. You are everything to me."

"Oh." Calla grabbed her by the collar and pulled her close, pressing their lips together. "I love you, Isolde."

The vampire held Calla by the back of her head. Her eyes were the only part of her that showed her age—the deep brown of fertile soil, dark windows to a soul that had seen more than Calla could comprehend. "I love you too." A tear slipped down her cheek. "I can't turn you, Calla. I can't do that to you."

Calla brushed the tear away with her thumb and looked at the hourglass. It gave off a faint glow, mocking them. "Do not think of my death, think only of the life we will have. We can see the world, watch the way it changes. We can do it together. You won't have to be alone. I'll be with you. Forever."

"I can't take you from the sun."

"You'll be giving me the stars." Another tear fell, and Calla kissed it away, brushing her lips over Isolde's cheek. "Please, don't argue with me anymore. This must be done, and if it must, I am glad it is me. I am glad it is you. Us. Together."

"Arguing forever."

"Yes. Arguing forever. Tonight, Isolde. We will do it tonight and then we will handle the rest. When we are done, we'll get on a plane and we'll find the nicest hotel. You'll teach me how to be a vampire and we'll fuck until dawn."

"Okay." Isolde nodded, her breathing ragged. "Tonight. I will call others, you will know you will never be alone in this world." She kissed her again fiercely, her tongue sweeping through Calla's mouth, her fingers digging into her skin. "Tell me again."

"I love you, Isolde. In this century and the next."

| Twenty Three |

FOUR hours later the house was full of vampires Calla had never seen before and every nerve in her body screamed to flee. She wasn't sure if it was her hunter senses, her human ones, or something entirely different, the last of her humanity bucking and kicking as it's time came to an end.

"Fuck." She gripped the bathroom counter and stared at herself in the mirror. She was being morose, even given the situation. Eternal life. How terrible could it be? And everyone was being kind, trying to tell her beautiful stories of immortality. Each word left Calla nauseous.

Someone knocked on the door. "You okay in there?" Biyu asked.

"Yeah. Coming." Calla splashed water on her face, careful not to get the floor-length gown she was wearing wet. She'd wanted to hate the dress when Molly had pulled it out, it was bright yellow with a strap across one shoulder and delicate orange beading on the bodice. She'd wanted to hate it, but then she'd slipped it on and the smooth fabric had brushed against her skin.

She took a last look at herself, the earrings dangling from her lobes, the red lipstick, the fake lashes. She barely recognized herself, but she looked beautiful. The dress reminded her of the sun. Vampires could not walk in the sun, but they could be awake in it. She would see it again. It was not her last sunrise.

She pushed the door open, and Biyu smiled. "I was beginning to think you'd flushed yourself down."

Calla forced out a laugh but it caught in her chest, and she was forced to grip a credenza for support. "Does it hurt?"

Biyu put her arm around Calla's shoulder, leading her towards the crowd. "Unlike Isolde, I wanted to be a vampire. I chose it. And..." She grinned, her eyes faraway, remembering a moment hundreds of years before. "It was not bad at all. My maker was a terrible man, but he was good at a few things."

"Okay." Calla nodded and brushed her hands down the front of her dress, smoothing it. She'd called her mother, who'd burst into tears but told her she loved her. She'd wanted to come, but Calla had begged her not to. If she saw her mother she would never be able to do this.

As she stepped into the room with Biyu, a hush fell over the room and suddenly dozens of sets of eyes were on her. Had she fought any of these vampires before? How many of these were the ones who got away? But they'd come on a moment's notice, Isolde was beloved. Calla would find a way to love them too.

"To a new link in the chain of the first lineage," someone said, raising a glass of blood and others echoed the sentiment until the clinking of glasses was all she could hear.

Biyu reached out and squeezed her shoulder then stepped away. What was she supposed to do now? Mingle? She wanted to get it over with, to feel the other side, to hopefully find some joy in it because at that moment terror was building inside of her. And the room was hot. It was too hot, and soon they would see the sweat on her brow, hear the fast pace of her heart, and know she was a fraud.

Through a gap in the crowd, Isolde appeared, and suddenly Calla could breathe again. The pressure that had been building in her head subsided, and she stepped forward. Isolde smiled and her breath caught again, but for all the right reasons.

"You look beautiful," Isolde said, stopping in front of her. "Maybe inviting all these people was overkill, because I do not want to share."

"I am learning you never do anything small."

Everyone was looking at them, vampires who had lived through things Calla could not even imagine. Vampires who had changed the course of history. But for Calla there was only one woman. Her blonde hair was swept back off her face and she had on one of her ridiculous hats, full of feathers and strands of pearls that looped and dangled. And her dress was low cut, showing off the pale skin between her breasts. Calla wanted to pull her close, bury herself in Isolde, taste every inch of her.

"Would you like to dance?" Isolde asked. She raised one of her hands and music began.

"I don't know." Calla's body might as well have been made of lead. "I'm not much of a dancer."

Isolde stepped closer, her lips brushed the shell of Calla's ear. "I need your hands on me."

And suddenly she was on fire. Her hands settled on Isolde's hips and centuries with her did not seem like enough. Calla had spent her whole life fighting, bouncing between lovers, never settling down long enough to feel anything real, and then Isolde had swept in and torn down everything she thought she knew, turned her whole life on its head.

Together they danced, spinning in each other's arms. Other couples joined them, human companions mixed in with the vampires, and Calla did not want to be a hunter anymore. She did not want to cause pain; she wanted this, a lover in her arms, her feet light on the floor.

Isolde's hips moved, pressing into Calla as the tempo increased. "You really do look beautiful. The great artists would have fought and killed for a muse half as gorgeous as you."

"When I said tonight I did not think you would get such a crowd, and I must admit, I hate them all. I want you alone."

"Do not worry about any of that. You have me and we will have time. We can start soon, but I needed this last time. I needed to remember how it felt." Isolde laid her head on Calla's shoulder, they swayed together though the song was a waltz. Others spun around them, but Calla and Isolde clung to each other until the final notes died away.

"Are you ready?" Isolde asked.

"Yes." Calla lied, though weeks could pass, and she did not think she would ever feel ready. But she would marry the night, become its bride and then she could have a thousand more dances. Then the others would leave, and she could pull Isolde to bed and not get up until the weather was warm.

Everyone cleared a path and Isolde started to move, but Calla seized her, kissing her roughly. Fangs scraped against her lips and Isolde's fingers tangled in her hair until they pulled apart, chests heaving.

Calla slipped her hand between them and took Isolde's, weaving their fingers together. Hand in hand, they walked through the crowd, like a bride down the aisle or a prisoner to the gallows, until they were in one of the sitting rooms.

All the furniture had been cleared away except for one velvet fainting couch and the hourglass, its last drop destined never to fall. Calla could feel its magic against her skin, more desperate than it had ever felt before, as though it knew its final moments were upon it. "Do they have to be here?" she whispered, looking around. She'd known New Dunwich was full of vampires, she'd worked in the city her whole life, but this felt private. Something between her and Isolde.

"Of course we will not stay. The turning is intimate," one woman with short brown hair said. "We never planned to stay, only to let you know that you are welcomed. Times have changed, and it is a blessing to welcome new vampires, to help them learn and make sure they are not lost in the world as so many of us once were."

Calla smiled. "Thank you."

"Of course. Isolde has served us over the years, we owe her the world. We will make sure your transition is as smooth as it can be." She snapped her fingers over her head. "Come on. Give them space. You were all on the precipice once." She winked at Calla and led the others out of the room. Biyu was the last to leave, and she pulled the door closed behind her.

"Sorry for ruining the show," Calla said.

"Nothing is ruined." Isolde's voice shook. "I'm—"

"Don't apologize." Calla silenced her with a kiss, running her tongue over the tips of Isolde's fangs, then moved lower, kissing the exposed skin of her chest, trailing her kisses lower until she was on her knees, looking up at Isolde. Her skirt was slit up the side and Calla ran her hand up her leg until she felt the lacy fabric of her underwear. She yanked them down.

Isolde moved with vampire speed. For a moment Calla was weightless, her body manipulated through the air, then she was on the couch, and Isolde was on top of her, her skirt bunched around her waist, her hat fallen to the ground.

Calla reached between her legs, finding her wet. She brushed her thumb over Isolde's clit, making her squirm, before she slammed two fingers inside of her and Isolde lurched forward, bracing herself with her elbows on either side of Calla.

Pulling her hand free, Calla flipped Isolde over and pressed inside of her again. She could not think of what came next. She kept her eyes on Isolde's face as she pushed into her again and again, her fingers curved, her palm against Isolde's sex. Her legs fell open and Calla stopped, bringing her soaking fingers to her mouth. She licked them, one then the other.

"Calla."

She shook her head. "Don't talk, Isolde." She pulled her dress over her head, and the fabric ripped. "I changed my mind." The vampire went still beneath her and Calla shook her head.. "Not about that. About this. I thought I wanted to fuck you, but I want you to fuck me." She took Isolde's hand and brought it to her throat. "Fuck me until I'm dizzy, until it hurts, and then turn me."

"Calla..."But her fingers tightened until she was gripping her chin.

"Do what you wanted a moment ago." And once again Calla was on her back, the vampire on top of her, pulling her dress over her head.

Isolde trailed her nail across Calla's cheek until her hand was again at her throat. Her jaw was set, her eyes dark and heavy. She tightened her grip, while her free hand grasped Calla's breast, she took her nipple between two fingers, pinching hard enough that Calla inhaled.

Calla dug her fingers into the velvet upholstery of the couch. Her eyes fluttered, but she kept them open. There was a change in Isolde, and hunger twisted her features.

She let go of Calla's throat and lowered her mouth to her breast, tugging at her peaked nipple with her fangs until teeth pierced flesh. While she licked away the blood, her hand made its way down Calla's abdomen and then between her legs and Calla pressed into her, desperate for friction.

Isolde obliged, pressing her thumb against Calla's clit, hard circles that left her panting. "You taste like fear and desire."

"Then don't hold back." Calla grabbed a handful of Isolde's hair and yanked her head up. "A lot of vampires have tried to kill me. You're the first that will get to."

Isolde smiled and there was blood at the corner of her lips. Calla's blood. Isolde entered Calla with a single finger. She added another. And another. Each thrust harder than the last. Calla's world condensed, there was only this room, this woman on top of her, the orgasm building in her abdomen.

Isolde lowered her head, she flicked her tongue across Calla's clit and put her free hand behind her, grabbing her ass and pulling her closer. Devouring her.

And then she did. Isolde sunk her teeth into Calla's thigh as she buried herself inside of her, and Calla clenched, coming around Isolde's fingers as she screamed her name.

Isolde looked up, blooding dripping from her chin onto Calla's stomach. She brought her wrist to her mouth and bit into it. Blood flowed down her arm. They were covered in it, more blood than Calla had ever seen. It stained the couch crimson. "Drink, Calla. You will be my first progeny, my eternal lover."

All trepidation long gone, Calla reached for her arm and brought it to her mouth. Magic sparked on her tongue, its fizzy tendrils filling every inch of her. Isolde threw her leg over Calla, grinding against her, and sunk her teeth into Calla's neck, their bodies writhing together, a tangle of limbs and slippery with blood.

Until someone ripped them apart.

| Twenty Four |

ISOLDE slammed into the wall before Calla realized what was happening. Gus stood above her and the screams of people below finally reached Calla's ears. She tried to push herself up, but her arms were weak, she'd lost too much blood. She'd been dying. And now she truly would.

She laughed, and Gus recoiled. She knew what she must look like, her teeth covered in blood, bleeding from her neck, her breast. She was every bit the beast he had been pretending she was.

"How did you get in?" But he'd managed everything he'd wanted, yet she'd still underestimated him. Time and again. She'd been unable to reconcile the monster he was becoming from the bumbling boy he had once been. He'd proven himself to her, but she'd turned her back on him each time, sure it was a fluke.

Saving Isolde should not have been her focus, she should have found him, made sure he was dead. She'd pay for her mistake with her life.

"There are plenty of humans willing to spend a few weeks endearing themselves to a vampire to earn their trust. It was easy to get in. You never learn, you never have." He grabbed her by her hair and pulled her to her feet. She tried to see beyond him, to see Isolde. Where were the others? But all she could see was Gus, the way one of his front teeth was crooked, the way his dark hair fell into his eyes.

He could have had another girl. He was handsome, tall and strong. But he'd hated her for turning him down. Hated her for being the one thing he couldn't be and the one person he couldn't have. A hunter who would never love him.

At the edges of Calla's vision, darkness creeped in. The night wasn't supposed to go like this. They'd been safe, surrounded by vampires and all the security of Isolde's estate. She blinked, trying to clear her vision. "Please."

"Please? You were going to be one of them, Calla. A fucking bloodsucker." He spat on her and it dripped, sticky and wet off her face and onto her bare chest. "So you'll die like one of them." He pressed her into the wall, and she could feel Isolde at her feet. She prayed some of the vampires had gotten away. She'd never thought he had enough numbers to get in here, but he'd played her. He'd dragged her around the Council building, letting her see what she wanted to see, a few weak hunters, a mockery of what they had once been. All the while he'd been plotting, keeping the real fighters away from her.

She reached for the side table, her fingers brushing over the hourglass, but the top was too wide, she couldn't pick it up with her fingertips. Gus's eyes followed her movement. A smirk pulled at his lips.

"What is this?" He let go of Calla to pick it up, and she fell to the floor beside Isolde.

The impact made her blurred vision worse. She could feel Isolde's body pressed against hers, but there was no movement. How could she be dead? Vampires didn't just die from impact. She tried to shake her, but her arms would barely respond to her demands.

"I said, what is this?" Gus crouched down beside her, holding the hourglass. She'd gotten so close. She'd almost done it.

"Fuck you." Calla looked up at him, and to her horror and amusement the last drop of blood dropped, ever so slowly, towards the bottom. Gus had no idea what he held, must be unable to feel the vestiges of magic running through the hourglass, because he raised it. The last thing Calla saw was the final drop of blood meeting the others as he smashed the hourglass over her head. And this time it broke.

The pain was dull, all of her senses losing their sharpness, but she could feel the glass and blood raining down on her. Maybe she should fight, maybe she could try to get away, but it was too late. Isolde would die along with Beatrix and Molly and Eleanor. So Calla let her head slump, breathing in the smoky scent of Isolde one last time. Calla could have loved her forever, could have built a beautiful life with her. At least they would die together.

Gus stood again, reaching into his back pocket and pulled out a stake. Calla remembered the way they used to feel in her hand, the comfort of the weight of the wood as she brought it down. She knew how it felt when it pierced flesh.

But she didn't know how it would feel as it pierced her own. The pain was terrible, sharp and deep. He must be at her heart, she felt her bones crack, but the pain didn't stop. She screamed as her vision went dark, but she heard no sound. With one hand she managed to reach for her chest and—

Calla Falling | Tallie Rose

| Twenty Five |

"CALLA."

"Calla."

"Calla, please!"

Someone was shaking her. That couldn't be right. She was dead. A stake had pierced her heart. She'd felt it go in. Felt the life slip out of her.

Her mouth was gritty, and she was shivering, colder than she'd ever been. But if she was thinking her heart must be beating. Which was odd. Everything was odd. Opening her eyes proved nearly impossible, but when she finally pried them apart they filled with tears at the sight of Isolde crouched over her.

"Calla, you have to get up. Something is happening." Isolde was wearing her ruined dress, she was drenched with blood and her face was pale. White as a ghost was the expression, which was funny. Were they ghosts? Was this the afterlife?

Far away, as though through water, there was a strange humming noise that Calla couldn't identify. She pushed herself up until she was sitting against the wall and looked down at her chest where there was no gaping hole, only a smooth white scar. "Am I..." She reached her hand up to feel her teeth. They were the same as they always were.

"I don't think so." Isolde grabbed Calla's dress and helped her pull it over her head, her hands warm against Calla's chilled skin.

Warm hands. "Isolde..." She looked at the ground, where shards of glass glittered amongst the splattered blood. "I'm alive and..."

"I think I'm alive too, Calla. I think I'm human." A smile broke across her face, her brown eyes sparkling and she grabbed Calla and kissed her. "The magic saved you, and I think it saved me too!"

Across the room, the door creaked. "Boss!" Beatrix said. Her eyes were wide and there was something about her, something changed. "You need to look outside and—are you okay?"

"I think so." Isolde stood and pulled Calla with her. Her body was waking up, each nerve tingling, but as far as she could tell she was whole. They rushed to the window and pulled the curtain aside. A glittery web of what must be magic surrounded the estate. It sparked teal and violet against the night sky emitting a humming sound with each sparkle.

Before Calla could get her fill of the beauty of the magic, Beatrix grabbed her by the shoulder and spun her around. "I think I... I think I'm a witch." She held up her hands where the same sparkling light that surrounded the estate swirled in her palm.

"I think Isolde is a human."

"Fuck."

"Bea, where is Gus?" Isolde said, urgency lacing each of her words. "What is going on out there?"

"It's a fucking mess, but I was hoping you'd be up." Beatrix looked between the two of them and a blush spread across her cheeks. "We had headed to the front of the house to give the two of you privacy when they broke in. It was one of the guards. They must have bribed him because they just walked in. It was chaos, everyone was fighting and then all the vampires just went down."

"Talk and walk." Isolde snapped her fingers and headed out into the hallway. Outside the room looked almost normal except for the trail of blood leading to the staircase. Gus must have thought they were both dead and left to join the fight.,

Beatrix followed the blood to the stairs. "We were all fighting, and I really thought the vampires would win, but then I got all tingly and all the vampires just... fell over. I thought we were going to die for sure but Molly figured it out. She was incredible. She blasted one of them with her light. A few of them ran off then, but the rest attacked us harder and it was just us. I managed to fight my way through them, which was terrifying by the way, and then used one of the passages to get here. I had to check on you." She paused for a moment, a strange look on her face and then threw her arms around Isolde. "I'm so glad you're okay."

Isolde awkwardly patted her on the back. "I'm also glad you're okay." Over Beatrix's shoulder, Isolde stared at Calla. There was so much to talk about, so much devastation and happiness to process. But they'd died, and Calla did not think they would come back if they died a second time.

Something crashed below them, and the two women broke apart. They sprinted down the stairs, following the noise. Outside the library Calla saw the first signs of the battle. Books were scattered about, their pages torn and strewn across the room. One of the ladders was on its side. Vampires and newly formed witches battled against the hunters that had come with Gus.

Self loathing almost creeped in. Calla could have stopped this. She'd been trained to fight, to never underestimate her enemies, but she'd done just that. She'd screwed up, bigger than she ever had before. But she could make it right. She could end this. Today.

Beatrix sprinted off to join the others, and Calla turned to Isolde. Despite their second chance, Calla knew they may never see each other again. This moment might be all they have. "I love you." She took Isolde's face in her hands and kissed her forehead. "Be safe. If you are human, you do not have the strength you are used to."

"I love you too. This is not the end of our story." With a final squeeze of her fingers, Isolde broke apart from her.

Calla scanned the room. She flexed her hands, hoping she still had her hunter's strength. Someone had dropped a stake, and she grabbed it. Whatever had happened, she was still Calla Chase, and the wood felt right in her hands.

Around her the fight continued, and she pushed through. Hunters battled newly awoken vampires and witches tested their new magic. Books exploded off a shelf and Calla ducked. That was not her fight. She had one target, and she was determined to find it. Gus knew nothing of leadership, though he'd been raised for it his whole life. His birthright had given him a spot on the Council, but no one had taught him integrity or wisdom. He had led these people to their death for nothing but pride and resentment. This fight was not against vampires, he could have fought them anywhere. This was personal, a vendetta against Calla, and all around her people were dying for it.

She tried not to look at any of the faces she passed, recognizing too many of them. People she had grown up with, eaten meals with, but their names still played through her head. She had to kill Gus. She had to end this.

Someone rushed at her, and she tried to move, but their fist glanced off the side of her head. She shoved the stake in her pocket and straightened herself. "Emory."

"Calla." There was a snarl on the hunter's face.

"Don't do this." She swung, but it was just a ploy. He ducked, and she kicked out, tripping him. He lurched forward bringing her down with him.

He punched at her again, and she twisted away. His fist slammed into the floor and he screamed. She used the movement to her advantage, flipping him over and pinning him down. But she didn't want to kill him. She couldn't. He was like her, used to following orders. In another life, she might have been him. So she hit him instead, once then twice. She screamed for help. She hit him again. His nose broke under her fist.

"Calla." Isolde was at her side. "We're holding them in the training room. I don't want a massacre. Beatrix!"

"Fuck you, vampire," Emory said around the blood in his mouth, but his eyes were unfocused. Calla doubted she was the first person who had hit him today.

"Not quite." Isolde grabbed him under one arm and Beatrix grabbed the other. "Miss the strength already."

Calla pressed her lips to Isolde's cheek, but there was no time for anything else. She still had to stop this. "Gus!" She screamed, moving deeper into the library. "Gus! Come out and play."

The fighting grew thinner as she moved deeper into the library. Had he run off like the coward he was? But something drew her forward and she kept moving. "Gus! You can't hide forever."

She rounded a corner and there he was, Molly at his feet. Sweet Molly, who had been the first to welcome Calla, was bleeding out on the floor.

Not Molly. Calla had come to terms with so many things, but that she could not abide. She would not lose Molly. Her chest rose and fell, but barely. She needed medical attention. Calla would make sure she got it. There would be no more death but one. "This is it, Gus. Just me and you."

"You died," he whispered.

"Not quite." Calla did not want to step on Molly, but she had to act while he was still stunned. She pulled the stake from her pocket in a swift movement and advanced. And just as she had hoped, he retreated.

Calla knew the library better than Gus. She lifted the stake in her hand and drove him back, towards the alcoves that lined the inner walls. She had the upper hand, there was blood at the corner of his lip, a bruise turning purple across his cheek, and his shirt was askew, revealing slashed wounds across his chest. He'd been fighting, he was tired.

"Call off your henchmen, and I'll allow you to be arrested. You don't have to die here, Gus."

"I'll be a martyr." He took another step back, not looking where he was going. Only feet until he was trapped in an alcove and he wouldn't be able to fight his way past Calla again. The first time he'd beat her he'd had numbers on his side, the second she'd been nearly drained of blood. Now it was just her against him, and he'd never win that fight.

"No, you won't. You'll be a fool. You'll be what the vampire rights movement points to when they say they aren't the aggressors, humans are. They'll make a mockery of your corpse and I will help them. Every step of the way."

His back hit the wall, and he stumbled but stayed upright. "What happened to you? We could have run the Council."

"I never wanted you, Gus. I never even considered the offers you made me. You are a small, weak little man who hides behind dogma that you don't even understand." Her body heat had warmed the stake. She took a step closer, she could see the sweat on his upper lip. "Isolde is human now too. We'll grow old together." She lifted the stake, turning it over in his fingers. "Last chance to live, Gus. Take the offer."

He spat in her face.

And she drove the stake home, through his soft skin and hard bone until it met the pliant muscle of his heart. She blinked away her tears as blood seeped from his chest, and his scream died on his lips. She stepped back as his body lurched forward, the stake still clutched in her hand. So many vampires had died at her feet but Gus was the first human.

Dead. Unmoving. Still. And unlike Calla he would not come back. No rebirth. No forgiveness. Just the end of a man more hateful than she had ever suspected. A man who had tried to kill her.

She took another step back, blood dripping from the stake to meet the growing pool on the floor. The house shuddered, and the glow that had been enveloping it was gone, plunging them deeper into darkness.

"Calla." Biyu touched her shoulder.

She turned, almost giving into tears before realizing she did not yet have that luxury. "Molly! She needs help."

"Of course." She knelt beside Molly. "Go get your girl, little human. I can take care of this."

Once Calla had believed in so many things, mostly that she was doing the right thing. Humans against vampires. Day versus night. Now,

224

she tore through the library, slipping on ripped pages slick with blood, screaming Isolde's name.

Her heart skipped a beat when she spotted her, her golden hair red with blood, her dress destroyed, covered in bruises but alive. Alive and human. Calla leapt over a fallen chair and pulled Isolde into her, breathing in her scent, still smoky and ancient, as if all the parts of her had not yet heard of her change. "I love you." Her voice was muffled by the warm skin of Isolde's neck.

"I love you too." She pressed a kiss to Calla's head.

Before Calla could respond there were sirens and the house was once again lit from outside, this time blue and red. "Know any good lawyers?" Isolde winked.

"Let me do the talking," Biyu said. Molly, alive, though pale, was at her side.

"We'll do it together," Calla said, putting aside her urge to lie down on the floor and go to sleep for a decade. Despite what she had told Gus, this was bound to be a disaster, and she was done with disasters. She wanted to move forward.

"Okay. You look like hell though and cameras will be here soon."

"It is what it is." Calla had spent her whole life convinced she was fighting for something good, creating a safe place for humans to live. Maybe she could actually do that. She had no delusions that all vampires were like Biyu and Isolde, there were still predators. There would need to be laws, speeches in front of congress, social media campaigns.

Everything was just getting started, and Calla was done letting life pass her by, done taking orders and doing what she was told. She wanted to help, to be a voice that so many people needed. So, even looking like shit, covered in blood in a destroyed dress, she wanted to be there when the camera crews showed up. The movement would need a face and Calla thought hers might do the trick.

And so, emerging out into the yells and flashing lights, that's exactly what she did.

| Twenty Six |
One Year Later

"YOU can't wear that."

Calla narrowed her eyes as she swooped in to kiss Isolde on the cheek. "One, when has telling me what to wear ever worked? Two, you've got half a bird on your head, so please curb your fashion advice."

"There's a stain on the ass." Isolde leaned over the vanity and pulled out a tube of lipstick. "But, by all means, do what you want."

Calla spun in a circle like a dog chasing its tail, trying to see her rear end where there was a faded but visible grass stain. "Thank you." She slipped her pants off and went back to her closet. "I'm so nervous."

Isolde's arms slid around her middle and she rested her chin on Calla's shoulder. "I'm so proud of you, baby. I know Biyu will never say it but she is too. It's not every day someone gets invited to speak at a summit of world leaders." Isolde kissed her neck.

Desperately Calla wanted to lean into the kiss, but if she didn't leave the house in the next fifteen minutes she was absolutely going to be late, and like Isolde said, it wasn't every day she got to talk in front of world leaders. She'd had a plan, and she'd done it.

She knew every nation wouldn't agree to the rights she had laid out for vampires, nor would all vampires agree to their part—namely only drinking from willing donors, but it was a start. Not even a start, a great middle. A big achievement. And leaders were going to sign off, there was going to be groundwork. And her fucking name would be on it.

227

In every news article, her name would shine and later be entered into textbooks. *Calla Chase.* The thought rose goosebumps on her arm. A year later and she could not be more thankful she had not turned into a vampire, but she was still going to be immortal. No one would talk of the vampires coming out without her name coming up. The hunter who stood up. The hunter with a vision.

They had never figured out exactly why she hadn't died, why Isolde had turned human. Maybe that had always been the purpose of the hourglass. But there was a little more magic in the world, a little more hope. Beatrix was leading that charge, working with scientists to figure out if a true cure was even possible. So far they hadn't found it, but Calla knew it was out there. If Isolde could be human, so could every vampire who longed for the sun.

"Earth to Calla." Isolde spun her around, her fingers splaying out across Calla's ass. "Blue suit, striped shirt. No tie, obviously. The earrings I got you for Solstice and the mauve lipstick."

"Really? The shirt won't be too much? Or should I wear a skirt? I might look more approachable in a skirt."

"Fuck that." Isolde yanked things from their closet. "Who cares about approachability?"

"We can't all have your confidence." Calla adjusted Isolde's hat, which had been knocked askew by their canoodling. "Are you still happy?" She asked the question too much, she knew that. But she couldn't stop. She worried about it constantly. She'd taken away her girlfriend's immortality. It was a big deal. Possibly the biggest deal. But Isolde never seemed to see it that way.

"Absolutely. Calla. This is something I never dared dream of. I know you worry about death and all that, but for me it's a blessing. I've had too many lives, too many heartbreaks. Now, I get to grow old surrounded by love. That's something special. And I really think your mom is coming around, so it's almost like I have family."

Calla laughed. "She's doing better than I expected." It was true. Delphine was certainly trying. She'd even gotten Isolde a candle for her birthday. Calla glanced at the clock and then looked out her window. "Shit, the car is here." She pulled on a new outfit quickly, taking Isolde's advice. "Ready?"

"To change the world? Absolutely." Isolde took her hand, their fingers intertwining without thought. A simple thing that had become a habit.

Calla straightened her back. She was ready to change the world, but whatever happened her world had already changed, irrevocably and forever, and she couldn't be more pleased.

More books by Tallie Rose

Sea and Flame Duology

- Sea and Flame
- Scale and Smoke

More Sapphic Fairytale Retelling

- Hecate's Hollow

Other Titles

- As Played by Gods

If you enjoyed this book please leave a review!